GW00570432

SCRATCH & CO.

H.K.P.

Magic Mountain

CAMP FOUR

Scoop's special camp

Red Rowan's Borran

CAMP THREE

Bivouac

spot at which Scratch fell into crevasse

CAMP TWO

climbing party caught in blizzard here and rescued by Red Rowan

CAMP ONE

Catterwaul Pike

Esk Hause

Catterwaul's Folly (for a drawing of this climb see end of Chapter Six. Note chockstone wedged in chimney: dangerous crack from which H.C. fell is above this on left)

HKP
CAT KINGDOM
EXPEDITION

BASE CAMP (note large mess-tent and flagstaff with Cat Kingdom expedition flag at masthead: see inset above for details of flag)

Sprinkling Tarn

Sty Head Pass

sheepfold where expedition stopped for night on way up ravine. Note trees where Tibs chased cuckoo on further side of ravine.

Styhead Tarn (Manx Scoop had his camp here. Note rocks under which rabbits hid from foxes)

Grain Gill

Stockley Bridge

THE ROUTE
OF THE
EXPEDITION

Seathwaite is the headquarters of the terriers, hardy little high-altitude porters.

Seathwaite

SCRATCH & CO.

THE GREAT CAT EXPEDITION

by

MOLLY LEFEBURE

With drawings by

A. WAINWRIGHT

MOUNTAINMERE RESEARCH
RISHTON · BLACKBURN · ENGLAND

Published by
Mountainmere Research
69 Harwood Road, Rishton, Blackburn,
Lancashire, England. BB1 4DH
info@mountainmere.co.uk
www.mountainmere.co.uk

New edition 2006
The right of Molly Lefebure

A catalogue record for this book
is available from the British Library

ISBN-10
0-9547213-1-4

ISBN-13
978-0-9547213-1-2

First published in Great Britain
in 1968 by Victor Gollancz

Printed and bound in Great Britain by
Titus Wilson, Kendal, Cumbria

For Daniel

CONTENTS

H.K.P.

CHAPTER ONE

THE ADVENTURE BEGINS

THE RABBITS, NEARLY two hundred of them, had travelled from all directions to reach Quayfoot Quarry from where, it was announced, the Great Cat Expedition up the Highest Known Peak (H.K.P.) would start.

Rabbits had come from everywhere; Borrowdale and St. John's, Ennerdale and Eskdale, Shap and Swinside, Matterdale and Mungrisedale, Seascale, Appleby, Newby Bridge. All were anxious to be engaged as Expedition porters. Some had travelled singly, some in parties, most had come on foot (for all were poor peasant folk), but a few had contrived to get lifts in tilt-carts or wagons, travelling at night over the old green quarry tracks and pack-pony ways, safe from the eyes of humans.

The rabbits, once arrived in the quarry, formed into groups; they lit little evening fires in sheltered nooks and cooked themselves simple suppers of sorrel soup, wild carrot and garlic. Some of them had brought supplies of crab-apple cider or elderberry-wine and as dusk fell the quarry began to echo with squeals of laughter, the music of harmonicas and accordions and the thudding of two hundred sets of feet thumping out the rhythm of ancient Border ballads.

The cats arrived in the valley late that same night, driving up in landrovers, their Expedition gear following in a convoy of lorries. The cats stayed as guests of the farm-cats at High Lodore; these cats were important animals in the neighbourhood, delighted to lavish hospitality and give every possible help to the famous mountaineers now come to Borrowdale.

The cats did not go near the quarry that night; but as they sat by moonlight in the walled field at the fell-foot, drinking sloe-gin and bleaberry-schnapps and talking of climbs and climbers, they could hear the distant thudding of the rabbits' feet, like rhythmic thunder far away in the hills.

The Expedition leader, famous old mountaineer and soldier Brigadier Sir Hywel Catterwaul (always known as H.C.), in his grey-whiskered fourteenth year but still a fine climber capable of going as high as many half his age, cocked an ear to listen. "Poor fellers," he said, his wise old face puckering into its celebrated roguery grin, "let 'em be happy now; they'll be singin' a different song when they find themselves staggerin' up Grain Gill with six-pound loads on their backs!" And, laughing, he told the tale of how he and the late O. Slim-Bones (probably the greatest climbing cat in history) had pioneered the Cat-and-Mouse Crack on Middlepaw Buttress each carrying a mousetrap. "As a joke, y'know. I mean Cat-and-Mouse Crack, rather nice, y'know; it was O. Slim-Bones's idea. He was always so full of fun." The other cats joined in his laughter, ready that night to find anything entertaining, even tales of O. Slim-Bones.

Next morning, very early, while the dew still flashed on the tips of the larches, the cats went down to the quarry to inspect the rabbits and select sixty of them as porters. The day had dawned fine and clear; new young bracken shoots were appearing, coiled spring-like, on the lower mountain slopes, blue-bells spread the ground of the valley copses. Cuckoos called in every direction.

"Nasty bird, the cuckoo," said old H.C., as he led the cats towards the quarry. "No sense of family responsibilities, y'know. Never liked the cuckoo. Tedious song, too, what?"

A blackbird, spying the approaching cats, dashed off giving his alarm to other birds in the neighbourhood. "Silly panicky things, blackbirds," said H.C. "Always thinkin' you're out to eat 'em. Personally I can't stomach 'em. Much prefer sparrers. Not so much meat on 'em, but a really good flavour. Sparrer-and-oyster pie; can't beat it!"

"Rabbits always think you're gonna eat 'em, too, come to that," said young Scratch Sharp. "What's the betting these porters will be shivering like jellies at the sight of us?"

"Doesn't do any harm to have 'em afraid of their betters," snapped H.C. "Doesn't do anyone any harm to respect their betters, come to that. Trouble with all the young 'uns today; no respect for their betters."

Scratch, who was walking immediately ahead of Oliver Simpkin, the Expedition's youngest member, turned round to give Oliver a giant-sized wink. Old H.C. didn't approve of Scratch and had not wanted him to be a member of the Expedition, for Scratch was a tearaway; indeed it was rumoured that he had first taken up climbing as a cat-burglar. The Expedition organizers, however, had over-looked this shady side of Scratch's character and had insisted that he should be a member of the Expedition because he was considered to be one of the finest climbers in Catdom, if indeed not *the* finest.

Oliver Simpkin, a charming young cat, a university student reading humanology, of whom H.C. approved as strongly as he disapproved of Scratch, replied to Scratch's wink with a broad grin. They were old friends and had enjoyed many climbing holidays together.

"Talking about feeding, sir," said Tybault Brightstone, the Expedition geologist, "I still think we'd be well advised to carry as little as possible in the way of food supplies and try to live off the land."

"Eating what, Tibs?" asked Dr. Thomas Black, the Expedition medical officer. "The porters?"

"No," said Tibs, laughing, "not the porters! No, seriously, these mountains are full of food: roots, shoots, edible fungi . . ."

"Good heavens!" burst in H.C., appalled. "Not that vegetarian fal-lal! Takes good red meat to get a cat up high peaks, my boy."

"Plenty of meat and fish supplies in these valleys, sir. Birds galore, field-mice, rats. Streams full of trout."

"And all we need is the time to catch them," said Felix Mouser, schoolmaster, photographer and poet.

"Precisely," snapped H.C. "We're here to conquer the H.K.P., not to rat-catch and trout-fish, let alone gather toad-stools."

"These local birds, what are they like?" asked Scratch.

"Feathered, my boy, all feathered," replied Tom.

"Wheat-ears, stonechats, yellow-hammers, ravens," said H.C., who was a keen ornithologist. "Ever seen a golden-eagle up here, Mouser?"

"No, sir," said Felix. "Have you?"

"Indeed I have," said H.C. "Saw one in Upper Eskdale with O. Slim-Bones in, let me see, must've been a good twelve years ago; we were doin' the Herring-Bone variation on the Fish-Cake Crack. It was Slim-Bones pioneered that one, y'know. Well there we were, half way up and me leadin', when I felt a great tug on the rope, wonder it didn't pull me off, and Slim-Bones sang out, 'Look, H.C., d'you thing that's a golden-eagle?' "

"Good old Slim-Bones," said Scratch, aside to Oliver. "Not his fault that old H.C. has survived to bore this Expedition to death."

"I looked up," continued H.C. who was rather deaf and therefore missed Scratch's remarks, "and there, circling over the Pikes, was this huge bird. Glorious sight!"

"Must've been, sir," said Tibs, politely.

"Slim-Bones was so inspired that he went up Breadcrumb Buttress upside-down to celebrate," said H.C. "Re-named it Golden-Eagle Buttress. Better name than Breadcrumb. Never cared for breadcrumbs; namby-pamby things. And *very* uncomfortable if you get 'em in your sleeping-bag."

"Very, sir," said Felix.

"Can't see why humans have to coat fish with 'em," said H.C. "Irrational. Still, humans are irrational; that's an established fact. No time for 'em whatever, meself. Dirty, smelly creatures, vicious and unintelligent. Well, here we are in the quarry. Good heavens, just look at all those rabbits! Nasty if that lot ran amok!"

Oliver began to giggle wildly at the thought of rabbits running amok. He had to drop behind to regain his composure.

The rabbits were seething and jostling in the open ground of the quarry, while two foremen scuttled about desperately trying to organize them into some sort of order. One of these rabbit-foremen wore round, goggle-like sun-spectacles and carried a lantern, the other was armed with a huge black umbrella. The rest of the rabbits were dressed in rags, with funny little peaked hats on their heads. They were all jumping, chattering and twitching, but immediately they realized that the cats had arrived, they froze into statue-still ranks.

"Call those two chaps here, Tom, and let's see what sense we can get out of 'em," said H.C., seating himself on a rock. Tom Black beckoned to the two foremen who at once came running. "This is Brigadier Sir Hywel Catterwaul, Leader of the Expedition." The two foremen bobbed their heads, their noses twitching madly with nervousness. The one with the lantern then introduced himself as Burrows; his mate with the umbrella was called Diggory. Poor Diggory bowed low to everyone in turn as his name was spoken, he almost got H.C. in the eye with the point of his umbrella which he held tucked under his arm.

"Tell him to watch out; I nearly got poked," said H.C. crossly. "What's the silly chump want with a brolly this fine weather, anyway?"

"It's for dusting their seats, sir, your honour," said Diggory.

"Seats? No seats here. What the deuce is the feller talkin' about? Does he mean he wastes his time dustin' these rocks?" snapped H.C. petulantly.

"It's for stroking their backsides, sir, your honour," said Diggory.

"Bringing them rabbits to order, sir, your honour," said Burrows. "They're a wild lot, yon rabbits."

"Aha, I understand you now!" exclaimed H.C. triumphantly. "A little spontaneous corporal punishment judiciously applied with an eye to anatomical structure, as O. Slim-Bones once said on a similar occasion. Eh, what?"

"Real witty geezer, Slim-Bones," said Scratch, under his breath to Oliver. "Someone oughter write down all his funny remarks before they're forgot."

"Well, on with the job, lads," said H.C. "Can't waste time coffee-housing. We need sixty good strong porters and the less time we spend on choosing 'em the better."

Now came an exhausting session of choosing the porters. The rabbits, at first exceedingly afraid of the cats, gradually lost much of their fear and unfroze, finally reaching the point where they were prepared to haggle without restraint.

"Don't choose him, sir. He's a scrawny one. Choose me. How's that for biceps, seesta?" Displaying a brawny right forearm. "Carry thy loads up Pikes and back in half the time of yon gaffer."

"Don't overlook me, your honour. Rabbit wrestling-champion for Matterdale, I am. Just thy ticket."

"Six pound load to Sprinkling Tarn? Feegh, I could carry Bowder Stone to Sprinkling Tarn if I had the mind!"

The task of selecting the porters went on all morning. By lunchtime the cats felt worn out. The early May weather was warm and dry, the sunshine poured into the quarry, reflecting back from the high rock walls, beating in heat waves upon the stones. The hot air shivered over the heads of the noisy rabbits and sore-tried cats. H.C. retired to a small patch of shade under a huge boulder; the sun climbed higher and straighter into the midday sky, the patch of shade dwindled to nothing, like a piece of melting ice. H.C.'s tail began to twitch at the tip, always a bad sign. Finally he rose and came over to Tom Black, who was surrounded by a swarm of babbling, squeaking rabbits. "These damn rabbits, worse than a crowd of perishin' sepoys," said

H.C. "I suggest we knock off for a drink and a spot of lunch, what?"

"Splendid idea, sir," said Tom. "I've never felt more in need of a catnip in my life."

The High Lodore cats had brought a delicious packed lunch to the cool green banks of the Derwent: smoked trout, cold mouse-and-mushroom patties, Cumberland sausages, cheese, and a beautiful golden sponge-cake. "Sponge, eh!" said H.C. "I love a good sponge-cake. Amazin' how few humans realize that cats adore sponge-cake. O. Slim-Bones, y'know, once had a jug of water poured over him by a female human for raidin' a larder and eatin' a sponge-cake."

Bottles of catnip and pipkins of cider were passed round. Presently H.C. stretched himself under a birch-tree, put a blue-and-white patterned cotton handkerchief over his face and began to make gentle sizzling noises between his whiskers. Felix Mouser said, "Well, he's off. Let's finish up the catnip, and then back to those perishing rabbits, I suppose."

"Who was that said I was off?" asked H.C., crossly and most unexpectedly, raising one corner of the pocket-handkerchief and glaring at Felix Mouser with a big yellow eye. "Hope you didn't think I was asleep, Mouser?"

"No, sir, of course not, sir," said Felix Mouser, hastily putting down the catnip bottle from which he was about to pour himself a king-sized nip.

"Afternoon naps are a stupid habit and a menace to serious mountaineering. So, by-the-by, is catnip tippling over one's luncheon."

"I couldn't agree more, sir," said Felix Mouser, attempting to hide the catnip-bottle behind his back.

"I like to stretch out after luncheon," said H.C., "close my eyes and have a few sweet thoughts." Whereat he pulled the handkerchief back over his face and soon began sizzling between his whiskers again. Felix Mouser waited a moment or two, then silently poured himself his king-sized drink and passed the bottle on to Tom Black. All the climbers helped themselves to catnip. H.C.'s sizzling turned into unconcealed snoring, interrupted now and again by odd little whistles. "Those sweet thoughts of his are hotting up," said Scratch.

"Marvellous old boy really though," said Tibs. "Hope I'm half as good as he is when I'm his age."

"Hope that when I reach his age I'll have more sense than to go on expeditions," said Scratch.

"I wish he wouldn't keep on so about O. Slim-Bones," said Oliver. "Grotty old bore, O. Slim-Bones must've been."

"Makes you wonder which of 'em bored the other most, dunnit?" said Scratch, lighting a cigarette.

"You two young chaps should count yourselves privileged to know H.C.," said Tom, rather severely. "He's one of the greats; one of the last survivors of the Golden Age of pioneer mountaineering, and a distinguished soldier into the bargain."

"Personally I think the old boy is the cat's-whiskers," said Tibs. "Wouldn't criticize him for the world, quirky though he is at times."

"Well, I wouldn't either, really," said Oliver, "only you know, he does keep on so about O. Slim-Bones."

"Well," said Scratch, "we'd best get back to that quarry and all them rabbits, nice as it is by this river."

The cats left the shade-dappled grass under the bushes reluctantly; H.C. continued to snore. They decided to let him be; to tell the truth not one of them fancied the task of waking him.

The quarry was hotter than ever when the cats returned to it, but the rabbits were loving the heat and had all stretched out full-length, sunning themselves luxuriously. Burrows and Diggory, sun-bathing on top of a rock, jumped alarmedly when they saw the cats and began agitatedly rousing the other rabbits; Burrows hitting them smartly with his lantern and Diggory prodding them with his umbrella. It took another good hour to finish selecting the porters. Then came the difficult task of arguing about how much they should be paid. Burrows acted as their spokesman; he kept repeating, "On behalf of my work-mates, might I put it to you that the sum you just mentioned, your honour, sir, is nowt but exploitation."

Finally, as the sun was setting behind Gate Crag, a price was agreed upon by all parties concerned. Tom Black ordered that a barrel of oak-apple ale be fetched from Rosthwaite to treat the sixty rabbits who had been engaged. The one-hundred-and-forty who were not needed were each presented with a threepenny bit, a bundle of parsley and a wad of rabbit-tobacco, with which they all seemed well pleased. They gave the Expedition three times three in rousing cheers and then marched away down Borrowdale in the bosky green gloaming, singing.

Next morning all the cats, bar Dr. Tom Black, went higher into the mountains to get acclimatised and to do preliminary climbs to tone them up in preparation for their assault upon the H.K.P. This mountain, never yet trodden by the paw of cat, not even yet named on the cat maps, soared above the neighbouring valleys; an enormous jagged ridge of rock leading to a series of savage summits, each higher than the last, the final summit being the Highest Known Peak in Catdom. So high were these final peaks that they still shone white with snow although upon all the surrounding mountains it had long since melted.

The climbers set off, carrying their own gear as part of their training discipline; tents, ropes, ice-axes, crampons, pitons, karabiners, sleeping-sacks, food, cooking equipment and so forth. Tibs Brightstone, however, firmly refused to take any food; he was going to live off the land.

The cats of Seatoller, at the head of Borrowdale, insisted on entertaining the climbers to a splendid breakfast. "Never get milk like this in the South," said H.C. "All bottled stuff there, y'know. Begin to wonder if the cows are made of plastic."

After breakfast the climbers said good-bye to their hosts and set off up Honister Pass. The sky was now grey; clouds drifted very low, oozing a thick wet mist over everything. At the top of the Pass the party paused for a breather, then struck up a rough track to the left climbing steeply on to the bare mountainside. Here Felix Mouser, who led them, quickly became confused. He took them round and round in the ever-thickening mist, until finally he had to admit what all the others had been guessing for some little while. "I'm afraid I haven't a clue where we are; any ideas?" But no helpful suggestion was forthcoming. Tibs, Scratch and Oliver were new to this part of the world. H.C. had been here with previous expeditions but had to admit that he, for the moment, was defeated; the mist had hidden all the landmarks. Head tilted back, grey whiskers twitching, he peered at the steep slopes above them, mist enshrouded and distinctly uninviting. "My instincts tell me to go up," he said at last.

"Kinky old instincts he's got," muttered Oliver. Tibs Brightstone said, loudly and cheerfully, "Up it is then, sir." And up they went.

Now came a really horrible experience; into black peaty quagmires sere with cotton-grass, up slippery scree, slithering over rainwet boulders, up ladder-steep terraces rough with old heather that grew higher than their heads, across becks tumbling with wild water. Finally they found themselves perched on a great mass of crag that thrust into the clouds, overhanging an empty space deep as a sea. The cats peered into the mist, unable to see a thing.

"Daft place to finish up in," growled Scratch.

"I vote we turn back and find another route," said Felix.

"My instincts are still to go up," said old H.C., peering into the clouds.

"O.K. for them with wings," said Scratch. "Bit hard on the rest of us."

"May I suggest a snack of Kendal Mint Cake and a pause for an appreciation of the situation," said Tibs.

"Splendid idea," said H.C. "Oliver, you've got the Mint Cake, I think."

Oliver gave everyone a piece of Mint Cake; they sat nibbling and staring into the pale furry nothingness of the mist. Nobody spoke.

Suddenly Felix dropped his Mint Cake. The hairs stood up on his neck, his whiskers and tail-tip twitched wildly.

"Ye gods, d'you see that?" he said, at last.

"See what, Felix old chap?"

"The most frightful face; all red with rows of teeth; rows and rows of 'em, sort of grinning at me. You never saw anything more awful."

"Where?"

"Why, there," said Felix, pointing with a trembling paw into the mist. "It was suddenly *there*."

"What sort of body had it?" asked H.C.

"No body, sir. Just a grinning face."

"Nonsense," said H.C. "Must have had a body. Unless it was the Cheshire Cat, and he was only a character in a book, y'know."

"Well if it had a body I never saw it," said Felix. "Simply came and went; a horrible red, grinning, tooth-filled face. Ugh!" He shuddered.

"Too much catnip yesterday luncheon, my dear boy," said H.C. genially.

"It was probably an Abominable Snowcat," said Scratch. "Were its paws on back to front?"

"All right, laugh," said Felix huffily. "But I know I saw what I saw, and whatever it was I for one certainly hope never to see it again. I vote we get out of here," he added.

"Then let's go up," said H.C. "When in doubt always go up."

"But up what, Brig?" asked Scratch. "There's no up left."

"Must be an up left somewhere," said H.C., rather gruffly. "We're in the heart of the highest mountain range in Catdom. Don't tell me we've arrived on the top of the H.K.P. without even knowing it."

At that moment the clouds parted like smoke and they found themselves staring down into a narrow little valley with a silver thread of water cascading through it. "That's the valley we're trying to find!" shouted Tibs. Then the mist closed again, the valley vanished.

"Well at least we know now where we ought to be," said Oliver. "Big question is how we get down there."

"Rope down," said Scratch, standing up and starting to remove the climbing-rope that he wore, sling-like, over his shoulder.

"Splendid," said H.C. "Nothing I like better than a good abseil."

In no time the cats had their rope belayed round a rock and were lowering themselves into space; their agility marvellous. They landed on a scree-bed; Scratch pulled down the rope and rewound it.

In this small, lovely valley surrounded by huge peaks and overhung by the enormous crag on which only a short time before they had been standing, the cats pitched their tents and set about cooking supper. Tibs prowled the banks of the little beck in the valley bottom and returned with two small trout, a water-snail, and what he said was edible moss; this was his evening meal and the others pulled his leg hard over it. They were all very cheerful, indeed noisily so, with the exception of Felix, who kept glancing nervously over his shoulder or stopping short, in the middle of frying sausages, to listen to nothing in particular.

CHAPTER TWO

MANX SCOOP AND WHISKEY BYLINES

Meanwhile, Tom Black, left in Borrowdale, sent fifty of the rabbit porters up the valley to Seathwaite, the headquarters hamlet of the terriers, the tough little local mountaineers who would take over as high-altitude porters when the rabbits, who were valley folk, could go no further.

The rabbits dawdled cheerfully over the journey up Borrowdale, stopping at farms and hamlets for gossip and to scrounge lettuces or drinks, loitering on the banks of cool rock-pools to smoke dreadful-smelling cabbage-leaf cigars, or merely sunning themselves wherever they happened to find a warm and sheltered spot. Burrows and Diggory, who were supposed to see that all fifty porters arrived at Seathwaite on time and in a reasonably sober condition, soon gave up the struggle; Burrows stole off to visit an old auntie in the Langstrath while Diggory, as soon as the sun grew warm each morning, found himself some secluded spot where he put up his umbrella as a sunshade and went blissfully asleep for the next eight hours or so. In the evening he strolled down to the road and thumbed lifts in order to catch up with the rest of the rabbits.

Tom Black, still at High Lodore, superintended the task of checking all the gear and supplies for the last time, buying reserve stocks of preserved eggs, dried fish, smoked bacon and ham and making sure that everything was in order for the great assault. As the things were finally checked the ten porters who had remained with Tom stowed them on to the lorries.

This was the last time that the Expedition would be in touch with real civilisation; here one could still send to a village shop for oddments like postage-stamps, boot-laces or chocolate biscuits. Once in the high mountains the Expedition would have to rely entirely on its own stores.

Tom, a methodical cat, had typed lists of everything: camping gear, climbing gear, high-altitude food, middle-altitude food, low-altitude food, all sub-divided into lists of climbers' food, terriers' food and rabbits' food. There were clothing lists, stationary lists, medical supply lists, lists of radio spares, landrover and lorry spares, film supplies, toilet accessories, miscellaneous such as tin-openers, corkscrews, fly-papers, safety-pins and string. He sat in a shady corner of the farm-yard, checking and rechecking his lists, trying to ensure that each group of things went on a certain lorry, and growing more and more muddled.

In the middle of all this an old landrover drove up with a very leggy, tough, hairy, chew-eared, battle-scarred Manx cat at the wheel. He was dressed in climbing-kit; looked a very old hand at a lot of things. A stack of gear was packed in the back of the landrover. On top of it sat a mongoose, wearing a turban and wrapped in a piece of striped blanket and looking ill-tempered.

The Manx cat climbed down from the landrover and came towards Tom with leisurely, yet deliberate strides. "Hi, there," he said. Tom looked up from his lists. "Afternoon," he said.

"Manx Scoop of *The Cat Times*," said the stranger. He took a carton of Gaullois cigarettes from his pocket, offered Tom one. "Thanks, I don't smoke," said Tom.

"You're Dr. Thomas Black," said Manx, lighting his cigarette. He inhaled thoughtfully, staring at Tom, who stared back. "Hywel Catterwaul about?" asked Manx.

"No, 'fraid not."

"Pity. Old friend of mine. I'd counted on seeing him," said Manx. Tom thought this unlikely. Manx didn't look like one of H.C.'s old friends.

Manx turned and called to the mongoose, "Ranjit Singh!"

"Sahib?"

"Tea."

"Immediately, sahib."

"For two."

"Precisely, sahib."

The mongoose unwrapped himself from the blanket, sprang down from the landrover and at once set about brewing tea with equipment from the landrover. Manx sat down on a low stone wall.

"How's it going?" he said.

"Well, you understand that I can't talk much," said Tom. "I mean, the *Cat's Courier* has bought exclusive rights to the story of this Expedition and it's simply not on for any member of this Expedition to give any information to a member of a rival newspaper."

"Quite understand that," said Manx pleasantly. "I'm just up here getting a general story, you know. Anyone from the *Courier* around?"

"They're supposed to be sending someone up to join us, but no one has materialized yet."

"Probably find yourself landed with old Whiskey," said Manx. "Can write, but doubt he can climb. Too damn fat. Know where I can get a few porters?"

"No idea," said Tom. "We had swarms of rabbits up here a day or two back, but we've chosen our lot and the rest have gone home."

"None in this valley?"

"You could try Troutdale. Though I believe we've taken all the able-bodied types from there."

The mongoose brought tea, and chocolate and almond cakes on a tiered silver stand. Tom raised his eyebrows at this unexpected elegance. Manx said, "I like a touch of civilisation, even in the wilderness."

The tea-set was porcelain, carefully unpacked from a padded wicker basket. The mongoose set the things out on a crisply starched, snow-white lace cloth. "Lemon or cream with your tea, sahib?" he asked Tom.

"Oh, lemon, please."

"Do help yourself to cake," said Manx.

Tom took a slice of chocolate cake. "It's delicious," he said.

"Ranjit's an excellent cook," said Manx. "Goes everywhere with me. Been with me ever since I covered that Bambu Kush cat-eating leopard story back in 'sixty-one. Ever come across a cat-eater?"

"No."

"Up here, of course, you get foxes. They occasionally eat cats. Dangerous creatures. You're armed, of course?"

"No."

"Trusting types, eh? Well, keep an eye open for foxes."

They chatted of this and that, then Manx took from his pocket a piece of paper on which was typed a neat list, "Anywhere round here where I can purchase a few last supplies?"

"There's a post-office at Grange where they sell pretty well everything. Another, perhaps not quite so extensively stocked, at Rosthwaite."

"I'll get Ranjit to nip down to Grange for me after tea," said Manx. "And after that, any odd item I haven't got I'll have to do without."

"Where, exactly, are you heading for?" asked Tom politely.

"The H.K.P. of course."

"Not with our Expedition," said Tom, pointedly.

"Lord no, dear boy; all on my oney-oh," said Manx. "I hate crowds."

"You realize, of course, that you haven't the chance of a snowball in Hades of making that mountain solo."

"Oh, I shan't mind if I don't beat you to the top. Climbing the H.K.P. isn't really the object of my visit here. My chief interest is in keeping an eye on you lovely lads and dear old Catterwaul. And in letting the world know when your feet finally patter across the snows of the sacred summit."

Tom said no more. Soon Manx called the mongoose to

him and spoke a few rapid words in Urdu. The mongoose then cleared the tea-things away, put Manx Scoop's shopping-list carefully inside his turban, got into the landrover and drove off down the valley.

Manx lit another cigarette. "Marvellously peaceful here."

"Absolutely," said Tom, staring at the sheaves of lists, the piles of equipment and stores, the lorries lined up across the yard and the ten squealing, scuttling porters.

Manx, too, surveyed it all with big amber eyes. "He doesn't miss much," thought Tom uncomfortably. "Dratted nuisance that he's turned up. He'll scoop the *Courier* if they don't watch out."

Manx, having finished his cigarette, excused himself and strolled away. Tom busied himself once again with his lists. Presently he came upon one which made no sense at all to him:

Razor blds.	1 pckt gr nts.
Tthpste.	Flints
Derwent toff.	Corn plstr.
12/4 stmps.	14 tins sardines tom sce.
3 pic pc.	? Dosh bck on bottles coke.

Tom couldn't recall making out this list and was still pondering over it when the mongoose returned in the landrover. Manx at once reappeared. "Well done, Ranjit Singh. You didn't waste much time. How d'you get on?"

"Both well and yet not so well, sahib. They had the safety-pins and the tin-opener, but seven dish-mops only they had, not the stock sufficient to sell us a dozen; also the fly-papers, only a dozen of these, sahib, instead of two dozen. And one very big ball of string."

"Safety-pins, dish-mops, fly-papers, string. Ye gods, Ranjit Singh, what's bitten you?"

"Sahib, such were your typewritten instructions."

"Typed instructions, tommy-rot. What the heck am I expected to do with seven dish-mops and a dozen fly-papers?"

Ranjit Singh felt round inside his turban and carefully

produced a piece of paper, folded very small. This he handed to Manx, saying, "What to do, sahib, what to do? Such were your typewritten instructions."

Manx unfolded the piece of paper, read it through rapidly, then gave an exasperated yell. "This isn't my list, dammit!"

Light dawned upon Tom. "May I see it a moment, Scoop?"

Manx handed the list over. It was Tom's list of miscellaneous items. Tom then handed Manx the mystery list, which had been puzzling him, 'Razor blds. Tthpste. Derwent toff.' and so on. "Is this yours, by any chance?"

Manx scanned it, then bellowed at Ranjit Singh, "You silly nit, you had his list, not mine! How in blazes d'you manage an idiotic thing like that, you perishing Tishbite?"

"Indeed, sahib, I absolutely understand myself unfortunate, for I see that a confusion arose."

"It did indeed! Now, thanks to you, you moron, I have seven dish-mops, a dozen fly-papers, safety-pins which I never use, not being a wearer of nappies, a tin-opener, of which I already have several, and finally a socking great ball of string big enough to tie up every damn mongoose in the Punjab."

"I'll buy 'em off you. I daresay we can always do with extra. And I can charge 'em up to the Expedition," said Tom. "Though you could charge them up to your newspaper come to that, I suppose."

"What, a dozen fly-papers, and safety-pins! My editor would think I'd gone barmy."

"Do you wish me to return to Grange and purchase the items on this other list, sahib?" asked Ranjit Singh.

"Yes, I do, and fast, else the post-office will be shut."

Ranjit Singh drove off in a whirl of dust; Manx strolled off to ogle a pretty young female cat, Tom went indoors to discuss the purchase of a flitch from the farm. The session turned into a lengthy one over mugs of fresh milk and toasted cheese-slices; when he came out of the kitchen back into the yard there was no sign of Manx, indeed there was no sign of anyone. Everything was very quiet and still. Tom shouted for the porters; he wanted them to load the flitch on to a lorry. No porters came. He shouted again. Still no porters. At last the pretty young miss emerged from a byre, tittering. "If you're shouting for the rabbits, they're all gone away," said she.

"Gone away, where?"

"With yon Scoop chap."

"Holy Joe Soak!" shouted Tom. "What a dirty trick!"

It was only too true. Manx Scoop had driven away with Tom's ten porters.

Tom rushed indoors, spitting with fury; the farm-cats immediately dispatched messengers to Troutdale, Peace How and Watendlath in an attempt to find more rabbits.

"Trouble is, there aren't that many rabbits round these parts nowadays. What we have got is an abundance of hares . . ."

"No hares," said Tom. "They're all mad. Hares never lead to anything but trouble."

He took a bottle of catnip and a glass, went into the orchard, sat under a tree and thought about his fiancée. They were going to get married when he returned from the Expedition.

Presently Tom saw a rather portly black-and-white cat coming towards him. "Bet that's old Whiskey whatever-it-is from the *Courier*," thought Tom. "He'll have to off-load some of that fat from his haunches if he hopes to accompany us any distance."

The black-and-white cat drew close, smiled genially, said in a deep, throaty purr, "Good evening. May I introduce myself? Bylines, Whiskey Bylines. You've probably already been warned by the *Courier* of my impending arrival." He held out his paw as he spoke. Tom rose and shook it. "Black. Dr. Black. The *Courier* people told us they were sending up a special correspondent, but they didn't name anyone specifically." He added, politely, "Nice of them to send such a distinguished member of their staff."

"Nice of you to say so, doctor," purred Whiskey.

"Sit down, have a drink," said Tom. "Oh bother, I've only got one glass. I'll go and fetch another."

"Not to trouble, dear boy," said Whiskey, lowering himself heavily into the grass. "If it doesn't worry you to have me drink out of the bottle, it won't worry me."

Without more ado he took a long swig from the catnip bottle, wiped the bottle's mouth carefully with his paw, then handed it gravely to Tom. "Anybody been up here?" he asked, casually.

"Depends who you mean by anybody. We've had quite a number of people up here—"

"Oh? Name them, dear boy, name them."

"The postman. Rabbits galore, Manx Scoop . . ."

"Wha-a-t?" yowled Whiskey, jerking very upright.

"Manx Scoop."

"Give me back that bottle, would you, dear boy? I find I need it."

Whiskey took another, very long, pull at the bottle. At last he spoke again.

"And what was friend Scoop doing?"

"Oh, looking around. Having tea. Shopping in Grange. And he pinched my porters."

"Dear old Manx. So like him."

There was a pause while Tom poured himself another drink.

"Is he still around?" asked Whiskey.

"No, he left suddenly, early this evening, with my porters."

"He didn't say where for?"

"The H.K.P. Where else?"

"Did you—er—talk to him? I mean, I hate having to mention this, but the exclusive rights of this Expedition story, you know . . ."

"My dear fellow I appreciate all that. And as a result I was discretion itself."

"Thank heaven for that." Whiskey took another swig at the bottle. "And you say he said he was going on the mountain?"

"Yes."

"Drat him," said Whiskey. "If I'm not careful he's going to mess up everything. Have me scooped before I can say pounce. If he's on the mountain, with a good strong pair of binoculars, watching everything that's going on—" He paused, sat thinking. "Or gets your porters spilling the beans." He paused again. "If he scoops me I'm done for."

"He's a most formidable-looking character," agreed Tom.

"Oh, he knows his way around. Never fear. A charming chap, but deadly as a rival, in every sense. Very." And Mr. Bylines took another thoughtful pull at the catnip.

"What sort of transport have you got, Bylines?" asked Tom after a bit.

"A very old Daimler I hired at Keswick."

"You'd better send it back to Keswick and come with me in my landrover to Seathwaite. That is, unless you have a lot of gear."

"Oh no. I always travel pretty light."

Next morning fifteen new rabbits turned up at the farm. Tom chose ten of them, Whiskey engaged the rest. His luggage consisted of a tent, cooking things, two or three big boxes of food, a sleeping-sack, tin mug, combined knife-fork-and-spoon set, toothbrush, two pairs of pyjama legs and one jacket, a comb, basic climbing-clothes such as a balaclava-helmet and an anorak, a hurricane-lamp, and a number of bottles of various lotions and patent medicines packed in a strong-looking chest labelled *First Aid.*

By evening everything was loaded on to the lorries. Tom and Whiskey had a lingering, pleasant supper with the farm-cats; the moon rose, the valley lay shadowy and mysterious, the distant lake slept, Lodore Falls could be heard tumbling and leaping alone amongst its trees and rocks. Tom stood for a moment by himself in the little garth behind the farm; he thought how romantic it all was. Then it was time to start the convoy. He called the rabbits; they climbed on top of the loaded lorries, perching amongst the bales and boxes.

The High Lodore cats came running to say good-bye; Tom and Whiskey had their backs slapped and their paws shaken until they felt almost in pieces. Then they got into Tom's landrover; the Lodore cats cheered, the rabbits cheered, Tom started up the landrover and in an instant he and Whiskey were off and rolling up the valley. One by one the heavily-laden lorries moved off after them; the High Lodore cats stood on the wall watching them go, their green eyes bright and staring and very large. Then when the last lorry had disappeared and the sound of the vehicles was a fast-dwindling rumble, the cats leapt lightly off the wall and went into the wood to hunt mice.

CHAPTER THREE

TERRIERS GALORE

THE ROAD UP Borrowdale ends abruptly at Seathwaite, a grey huddle of low stone buildings in the deep valley-head burrowing into the very core of the great mountains. It is a wild and lonely place.

Tom's convoy drew up there in the early hours of the morning, when the brief northern summer night was already lighting into another long day.

The climbing-cats were not there to welcome him; they were still absent on their acclimatisation exercises, but directly Tom and his train of vehicles drove into Seathwaite there was a violent din of yapping, yelping and barking and from every building in the place terriers came running. These terriers, natives of the high region of the District, were born and bred mountaineers; tough, hardy little animals who could walk and climb for miles on end over the rough passes and high peaks and never tire. They never felt the wet or cold, lived on the roughest, simplest food, were always happy, lively and full of good-humoured mischief, were loyal, brave and true. As a result they were greatly sought after as guides and high-altitude porters.

Now Tom and Whiskey slowly climbed down from the landrover while the dogs leapt round them and bounced upon them, keeping up a constant barking. "Good chaps, good chaps; delighted to see you and all that, splendid to be here and everything," said Whiskey mechanically over and over again, edging his way rather distastefully through the seething crowd of terriers; Tom followed, mewing politely. "Hello there, hello there. Marvellous. Marvellous." The farm-cats now appeared, strolling out of the front porch of the old farmhouse; they led Whiskey and Tom into the kitchen. The humans were still abed, although the noise of the dogs had stirred them and somebody opened a window and bawled, "Shut that row or I'll be down to warm ye!"

"Well-meaning chaps, yon terriers, decent at heart, but a dog's always a dog and there's no escaping that fact," said the oldest farm-cat. "Just as we cats are cats."

"Absolutely," agreed Whiskey. "Our ways aren't their ways, nor theirs ours; the two races are quite different and it's best to keep things that way."

"One has to have a certain amount of contact with them in the daily round," agreed Tom, "but it's a great mistake to try to fraternise beyond a certain point."

"Let's face it, they're inferior to us," said the old farm-cat. "It's true that this farm couldn't carry on without dogs; the shepherds depend upon them to round up the sheep and all that sort of work, but when all is said and done it's nothing more than labour of the lowest sort. A dog has to learn everything; trickwise; a dog can't think for himself. When they're well-trained, dogs seem, at first sight, to be highly intelligent; that's how human beings get taken in by them, you know. But, by gum, put an ordinary untrained dog down beside an ordinary cat and yon cat will have the dog outwitted every time!"

"Aye!" said all the other farm-cats in chorus.

"Indeed yes!" said Whiskey.

"Dogs may be daft," scowled Tom, "but for sheer pudding-headedness you can't beat a rabbit. Heaven preserve me from rabbits!"

Poor Tom! He was understandably fed up. The fifty rabbits who had gone up the valley in advance were supposed to be assembled at Seathwaite by now, ready and waiting for him, but all the way up the valley the landrover had overtaken little groups of rabbit-porters, dancing in the moonlight, or seated comfortably by the roadside eating onions and telling stories. Tom had bawled at them as he passed and they had leapt to attention and scuttled to cadge lifts on the lorries so that they would be at Seathwaite on time. The result had been that each lorry had toiled up the final stretch of road with a pyramid of rabbits swaying on it. Directly the lorries had drawn up at the road's end the rabbits had jumped down and had darted up the fell side amongst the rocks and ledges of Jenny Banks, where those who had arrived earlier had already set up a camp.

"Rabbits are O.K. so long as you keep an eye on 'em every blessed moment," sighed Tom. "But take your eye off 'em for a split second and you've had it."

"Pie," said the old cat. "That's all they're fit for, pie."

Meanwhile the terriers had squeezed into an old hen-house to have a brew of tea and a yap. "Pity it's a cat Expedition," said little Jack Russell. "Stupid creatures, cats. Now that last expedition we went with, that one over Coniston way, that was champion, that was. Boxers and bull-terriers, they were; a right grand lot o'chaps."

"Oh aye," said all the other terriers.

"Mind you, they had a rare lot o' trouble getting a permit to allow them into the Cat Kingdom to climb here," said Alec, the Border terrier. "The Queen of Catland, she's not over keen on allowing parties of dogs into these parts, to climb. If we weren't all natives, born and bred here, she'd have us out, I reckon. As it is, these cats always treat us dogs like second-class citizens. It's a scandal really."

"Oh aye," chuckled Bits, a dish-mop of a dog, whose snout, eyes and ears were totally hidden by hair. "Many's the time I've had a good bit of sport, chasing a cat. Off they run, then they turn round and spit at you, and call you an inferior; who's inferior to who, I'd like to know? The one that runs, if you ask me."

"Hear hear!" barked all the other terriers together.

"Never mind," said Yorky Boy, the Yorkshire terrier. "You can always laugh at 'em; there's no law against laughing at a cat."

"Bit risky though," said Pooks, the Sealyham. "For it makes 'em that mad, and a cat in a rage can be nasty."

"Most of the time they'll never let on they know you're laughing at 'em," said wise old Alec. "They lose dignity, if they admit they're being laughed at. And to a cat dignity is the most precious thing in the world."

"Aye," said Rabsie, the Aberdeen. "A dog doesn't like losing face, but if he does lose it he'll have the grace to grin; he'll see the funny side. But there was no cat ever yet born with a sense of humour."

The terriers, warm and comfortable after their tea, curled one against the other and went to sleep. The rabbits up the fell prepared sorrel salads for breakfast. The cats sat chatting by the big kitchen range. So all was peace for a while.

"By the way," said Whiskey, "have any of you good farm folk seen a Manx cat round these parts? A big leggy fellow, got a mongoose with him and, I believe, a few rabbits too."

"Aye," said a young cat. "Yon Manx came this way yesterday. He and the what d'you call him; looked like a big scruffy stoat . . ."

"A mongoose," said Whiskey.

"Aye. Had a turban on its head. They parked their landrover here, then walked up to Stockley Bridge and started up the Sty; there were ten rabbits with them, carrying a lot of stuff."

"Up the Sty Head Pass?" asked Whiskey.

"Aye."

Whiskey looked worried. He muttered, "That Manx will steal a march on me."

The next few days were hectic ones for Tom. He had the hard job of getting all the gear off the lorries and divided into loads for the rabbit-porters to carry. The result was chaotic. The rabbits argued about the loads, would not agree as to which would carry what and, indeed, behaved in the most tedious and tiring fashion, until poor Tom felt quite worn out. Whiskey did his best to help, but he was not very good at handling rabbits and anyway his mind wasn't really upon the work; he was worrying all the time about where Manx Scoop had got to and what Manx Scoop was up to. Manx Scoop became Whiskey's one thought.

He kept talking about Manx Scoop until Tom was perfectly fed up.

"Wonder where Manx is now?" Whiskey kept saying, turning to stare at the great black barrier of mountains closing the dale head.

"He won't get very high on his own," said Tom. "The H.K.P. isn't a solo climb."

"Wouldn't like to be up there by myself," said Whiskey. "Apart from anything else there are the foxes. I wouldn't care to meet a cat-eating fox. There've been some nasty cases reported in the Press recently of cat-eating foxes."

"Can't see any right-minded fox trying to eat Manx Scoop. He looks very tough, in every sense."

Whiskey glanced quickly and uneasily down at his own fat tummy and even fatter legs. He said nothing.

The rabbits jostled round, squealing. "Let me carry the blue tent!" "Me for the tinned peaches!" "I doubt those cans of squash weigh a ton." "Feegh, this load's more than six pounds, seesta. Every bit o' ten, I'd say." "Out o' my way; I'm carrying yon peaches!"

The day was close and sultry; Tom wiped his face round with his paw and sighed loudly. "Why did I decide to come on this Expedition?"

Suddenly they heard bagpipes; first in the thin distance, then skirling nearer. All the terriers began barking joyfully, running into the road as they did so. The rabbits and the two cats hurried to look; there coming down the road was a blithe little figure in a swinging kilt, a plaid over his shoulder, a Highland bonnet on his head, the bagpipes clasped to him as he almost danced along to the strains of *The Road to the Isles*.

"It's Hamish, it's Wee Hamish himself!" yelped the terriers, racing to meet the piper. There was a swirl of plaid and a skirl of the pipes as terriers closed gleefully upon Wee

Hamish, so that for a moment the little dog quite disappeared. Then there he was, marching up the road piping
loudly, with a cheering procession of terriers bounding
behind.

"Wee Hamish McCall, the most famous mountaineering
terrier of them all," said Tom. "Worth your while writing an
article about him, Whiskey. By all accounts he's a character."

Wee Hamish swung up the road with the terriers at his
heels; they all went into a barn and soon jubilant sounds
indeed could be heard coming from that direction. The
farm-cats looked disapproving. "Yon Hamish McCall. It's a
pity he doesn't go back to Scotland where he was born.
This side o' the Border could do without him."

"Where does he live?" asked Whiskey, getting out his
notebook, eager to gather information about a colourful
personality.

"In the Newlands fells; they can keep him."

"Where did you say he was born; Scotland?"

"Aye. His father was a West Highlander, so they say. His
mother was a Yorkshire lass with a French name; Fifi.
Makes you think, doesn't it?"

Whiskey was busy writing all this in his notebook. "And
what does this Hamish fellow do when he's not mountaineering?"

"Hunts."

"And when he's not hunting?"

"Mountaineers."

"Sounds a nice life," said Tom. "Better than spending
your days doling out pills to animals who have nothing
wrong with them except too much eating and not enough
exercise."

"Or writing for newspapers that end up as wrappings for
fried fish," said Whiskey.

The merrymaking went on in the barn for several hours.
When their work for the day was done the rabbit-porters
gathered round to listen, then started a party of their own

with a camp-fire and clog-dancing. The farm-cats fetched out a banjo and soon they were in full swing too, with Tom and Whiskey singing a duet, *The Owl and the Pussycat.* Then Whiskey sang *Take a Pair of Sparkling Eyes* followed by *The Road to Mandalay* and Tom sang *Oh Mistress Mine Where Are You Roaming?* and they had just started another duet, *Shoo Fly, Don't Bother Me,* when H.C. appeared followed by the rest of the climbing-cats. The duet ended suddenly. Everyone escorted H.C. and his party indoors, to give them supper and hear what they had to say about conditions in the high mountains.

"Conditions are pretty good, actually," said H.C. "Sparrer-pie? How perfectly splendid! Not too much snow, y'know; almost all melted; some still lyin' in the northern gullies. Sponge-roll and treacle? Oh I say! How did you guess that was my favourite?"

"By the way," said Tibs, laughing, "poor Felix wants to know if you have any Abominable Snow-Cats in these parts. He thinks he saw one."

The farm-cats roared with amusement. Felix looked sulky and presently got up, excused himself and stalked out. "Moody young chap, that," said H.C. "Don't altogether like the way he's been behavin' recently. Keeps lookin' over his shoulder; 'fraid he's started seein' Boggles."

"Who on earth is Boggles?" asked Oliver.

"Why, surely you've all heard Slim-Bone's famous story of the Boggle of Rosset Gill?"

"Oh yes, sir, we all know that one," said Tibs hastily.

Scratch said, "My mind still boggles at the memory of it."

"I've never heard it," said Whiskey. The other cats glared at him, except old H.C., who turned to him eagerly. "Haven't you, my dear feller? Why, there was this thing in white, y'see, comin' down Rossett Gill in the gloamin', y'know, and so everyone naturally supposed that it was a Boggle, although in actual fact it was someone, a practical joker, dressed up, y'know."

He paused. Whiskey started to laugh politely.

"But that's not the end of it," cried H.C. happily. "Not by half. Best part's still to come. My dear old friend O. Slim-Bones, though he was young then, I was young, the world was young . . ." His voice broke off, he sat staring sadly at nothing. Whiskey said, "O. Slim-Bones. Now who was he?"

"By gad!" bellowed H.C. very crossly, springing to life. "It's a fine kettle of fish when the *Courier* sends us a special correspondent to write about the biggest mountaineering adventure in history and he's such a nincompoop that he's never heard of O. Slim-Bones!"

"I'm not a climber, Sir Hywel," said Whiskey.

"I can see that," said H.C. rudely. "I hope you're not going to try coming with my party, Mr. What's-your-name; for we haven't got time to waste bothering with out-of-condition gossip-writers. I can tell you that for a start."

Tom hastily changed the subject. "Did you know that Hamish McCall had arrived, sir?"

"Wee Hamish?" cried H.C., looking happy again. "Now he's feller after my own heart, though he *is* a dog. Nice little chap! Fine little chap! Now, he'll have heard of O. Slim-Bones, that's for sure."

"Since he's climbed with H.C. on several occasions you can bet your life he'll have heard of O. Slim-Bones. And how!" said Oliver to Scratch.

"Shall I fetch him here, H.C.?" asked Tom.

"Please," said H.C.

Tom hurried to call Wee Hamish and soon the little terrier came trotting briskly. H.C. and he greeted one another with enthusiasm. H.C. insisted upon Wee Hamish sitting down to supper with them; Wee Hamish was in fine form and told tales about his hunting and climbing while H.C. told story after story about O. Slim-Bones. Wee Hamish howled with laughter at these, while H.C. was delighted with Hamish's anecdotes. So the two spent a very happy evening and never noticed that after a while they were alone in the farm kitchen together.

The next day was spent choosing a team of terriers to

accompany the Expedition. Hamish advised H.C. which terriers to take. "Have Alec. He's a fine wee mountaineer and verra steady. He'll no let ye doon in a crisis. And Rabsie, he's a bonny dog on a mountain too, and strong. Jack Russell, aye, take him along; he knows this country as well as any living soul and will never tire on a march. Yorky Boy y'must take; he's wee, but he's fine on rocks. Brat Wilson is another wee body ye canna leave behind; he can smell his way from here to the Solway in mist as thick as rum-butter. Bits; och weel, I grant he looks like one o'yon Beatniks, in bad need of a hair-cut, but he's a guid wee creature for a' that an' fine in the snow."

The terriers stood waiting to have their names called; they were all dreadfully excited; some of them trembled, one or two made high-pitched sounds to themselves like electric-light bulbs about to fuse. H.C. muttered to Hamish:

"What about those two little chaps sharing that chain-coupling; those two little black-and-tan fellers? They look a keen pair."

"Titch and Tiny? Och, aye, they're a fine wee couple: brothers. Tiny is a grand wee climber that never gives up on a mountain, however steep, while Titch is a bonny fighter; he'll fight anyone twice, three times his size, aye and beat him too. Take Titch and ye need have no fear of foxes."

"That's nine terriers, including yourself, Hamish. We need three more. Who else do you suggest?"

"Weel. I'd say Pooks, the Sealyham. He's a verra dependable dog and a verra cheerful nature; always looks on the bright side. And Sankey; he has the second-sight. And last of all I think ye'd be verra wise to take Moody; he's a braw wee dog, ye'll nae regret takin' him."

Thus the terriers were chosen. The disappointed ones behaved very well, though clearly they were downcast at not being selected. "Another time, lads," said H.C. "We'd take you all with us if we could, y'know; but it's just not possible. Twelve of you chaps is our limit for this show."

Now came the final hectic hours of getting the Expedition away. The climbers set off in advance with the terriers, making for Base Camp. The terriers, dressed in anoraks and carrying huge packs as if they were feathers, danced easily up the stony, steep track laughing and yapping with excitement as they went. This advance party started shortly after the sun was up; they would march for two or three hours and then have breakfast. The rabbit-porters were not ready to start until much later.

Whiskey rose with the crack of dawn; he had a long, confidential chat with Sankey and Moody behind the hen-houses. He then strolled back to the kitchen, while Sankey and Moody, shouldering their packs, exchanged a few brief words with Hamish and then hurried away up the Sty Head Pass. Nobody else saw them go.

The farm-cats walked with the main party of climbers and terriers as far as Stockley Bridge. Here they said good-bye and good-luck.

Tibs Brightstone and Tom Black had remained with the rabbit-porters. It took a long time to get these loaded and ready to march; finally they set off, in ones and twos at first, then in larger groups. Diggory and Burrows, not carrying loads, pattered anxiously up and down, Diggory using his umbrella now as a sunshade, now as a weapon with which to prod the porters, Burrows waving his lantern to emphasize the orders he kept shouting, but to which nobody paid the slightest attention.

At last all the porters were wending their way along the rough track to Stockley Bridge. Tibs and Tom strode off; Whiskey beside them, with his porters behind him. It was understood that if he couldn't keep up then he must drop behind and fend for himself as best as he could.

The sun rose higher in the sky. The light poured into the shadowy dale head; the dew-white fields by the river turned bright green, the mountains changed from inky-black to smoke-blue. The porters began singing in unison; a long, long song which seemed to have no ending. Stockley Bridge came into sight and beyond it the steep, narrow ravine of Grain Gill, leading into the heart of the highest mountains. "That's the way we go up," said Tom to Whiskey, pointing to the Gill. "Jolly good," said Whiskey, smiling gamely. To himself he muttered something different; Tibs, standing close behind him, thought it sounded like, "Oh my sainted aunt!"

CHAPTER FOUR

THE ARRIVAL AT BASE CAMP

THE BRIDGE SPANNED a very narrow rocky gorge filled with green and silver water, clear as glass, the green water lying deep and still, the silver rapidly tumbling and foaming. Beyond the bridge the stony track of the famous Sty Head Pass climbed over a mountain's shoulder and wound out of sight; to the left of the Sty another track led up the ravine of Grain Gill. This was the route the Expedition was taking. Manx Scoop had gone up the Pass, a longer way into the central *massif* but one more frequently used by travellers.

The porters loitered a few moments by the bridge and the cool water before turning up the ravine, chided by Burrows and Diggory. Tom, Tibs and Whiskey sat down on the bridge parapet for a cooler. Tibs drew very near Tom and asked, in a low voice, "Have you any chocolate?"

"Bit early in the day yet for chocolate, isn't it?" said Tom.

"I'm starving," said Tibs. "Be a pal."

"Didn't you have any breakfast?"

"Yes, I did, but I've got an awful lot of leeway to make up."

"Whatever d'you mean, leeway?"

"An awful lot of missed meals to make up for."

"Missed meals? Which missed meals?"

"While we were away acclimatising. The others took their provisions with 'em, but I lived off the country."

"And?"

Tibs glanced quickly at Whiskey to make sure he wasn't listening, then whispered, "I simply couldn't find anything to eat."

"Birds?"

"The birds, what few birds there were, proved impossible to catch. They sort of fluttered along in front of me, laughing; then flew off at the last moment. Maddening."

"Mountain streams full of trout?"

"I got two, midget-sized, the first night, and a sort of a snail. After that, nix."

"No food at all? What about the good old fungi, edible moss and all that?"

"There didn't seem to be any fungi. I think it's the wrong time of the year or something. There was quite a bit of moss, but you try living on moss, dear boy, for the best part of a week and see how you feel at the end of it. I say, *haven't* you any chocolate?"

Tom sighed and handed over a bar. "Eat it slowly, Tibs." Tibs nodded and gobbled it up. "Gosh, that feels better. I suppose you haven't an apple handy, or anything like that?"

"I have not got an apple handy."

"Small sliver of Kendal Mint Cake, perhaps?"

"Certainly not. Wait till we get higher." Tom stood up and reshouldered his rucksack. "Anyway, what's happened to *your* chocolate, Mint Cake, apples? You were given a ration too, weren't you?"

"I ate them before we started," said Tibs.

"My sainted puss! You have lost your self-control, haven't you?"

"Look, I'm hungry."

"Your own fault. You kept mewing on and on about living off the land and all that jazz, now you see what an idiotic idea it really was."

"I feel quite weak."

"You'll survive."

"How nasty and unsympathetic you are. I shan't be one of your patients."

"Nothing delights me more than to hear you say that, old chap."

Tibs scowled as he picked up his rucksack; then thought

better of it and tried a wheedling tone. "Just one piece of Mint Cake. To keep me going. Just one bit. Please."

"Oh, very well then, and against my better judgement."

Tom broke off a piece of Mint Cake from a packet he took out of his pocket. Tibs snatched it and crammed it in his mouth. Tom said, "If you go on like that you will become one of my patients, and a lot sooner than you think."

"Rats," said Tibs. "Good Mint Cake never harmed anyone. I feel a new cat."

They started up the ravine. Whiskey walked in the rear; he puffed as he climbed; every other minute he stopped for a breather. Gradually he got left behind.

"Old Whiskey's making very heavy weather of it," said Tibs. "If he's like this now, what on earth's he going to do when we reach the really difficult stuff?"

At midday they halted in the shade of a large boulder and shared Tom's lunch, since Tibs had eaten all his. Whiskey caught up with them and sank wearily into the patch of shade too. "What a life! I'd like to see my editor sweating up here! Good grief, what a terrible part of the world this is! Not a flat piece of land in sight."

He took out a thermos-flask and drank a great deal of iced-coffee.

"Not very good for the wind," said Tom. "Don't forget you've a longish march ahead of you this afternoon."

"Too thirsty to care, old boy, too thirsty to care," said Whiskey.

"Aren't you going to eat your sandwiches?" asked Tibs.

"Don't feel like eating, old man."

"May I have one or two of them, then?"

"Do. Polish off the lot if you feel like it."

Tibs at once ate all of Whiskey's sardine sandwiches, his chocolate, a bag of apples and a box of cheese-triangles. These he found at the bottom of Whiskey's rucksack, into which he had delved shamelessly. "Don't tell me," said Tom who had watched this, "don't tell me that you aren't going to eat the actual box as well."

Whiskey lay dozing. He was not a happy cat when they woke him and told him that it was time to start moving again.

The ravine stretched in endless ascent. The rabbits, all valley folk, found this high upland country very uncongenial and their tempers began to fray and their spirits to flag as the path grew rougher and steeper, steeper and rougher, and the mountains crowded higher and higher and the air grew thinner and colder. Long before the evening shadows were stealing up the mountain faces, leaving only the peaks ruddy and shining, the porters were crossly asking Burrows and Diggory where they were going to camp for the night.

"Just a little higher, lads, not far now; one more haul, lads, and then you can make your camp-fires," sang Diggory twitching nervously.

"We shall want overtime for this!" squealed one rabbit. "Aye, and danger money too," said another. "What a way to treat decent rabbits!" cried a third.

At last they reached the sheep-fold where the Expedition was to halt for the night. The climbing-cats had already pitched their tents in the shelter of the fold; the rabbits built their fires and put up their ragged little tents, low and crooked, made out of potato-sacks and old table-cloths and goodness knows what else. When Tibs and Tom reached the camp the cooking pots were over the fires and the savoury smells rose on the evening air. Tibs went round sniffing happily.

Sankey and Moody had rejoined the other terriers; they were all laughing, joking and eating a meal of biscuits and old bones. When Whiskey at last came puffing and limping up to the sheep-fold Sankey greeted him with a few words; Whiskey said, "Later, there's a good fellow, leave it till later." The poor cat flung himself on the ground, examined his sore pads, called for his First Aid chest. "I can let you have some plaster, if you need it," said Tom, kindly.

"Thanks, doc, but I think I have just what I need right

here," said Whiskey. He unpadlocked the chest, took out a bottle labelled *Embrocation*.

"Shall I rub it on for you?" asked Tom, still trying to be helpful.

"No thanks, doc, I can manage," said Whiskey, standoffishly Tom thought. The doctor therefore left Whiskey to it. Tom found the tent he was to share with Tibs and settled down to make himself comfortable.

Tibs sat outside the tent, writing some geology notes. H.C. came by. "Caught your supper yet, Brightstone?"

"What?" gasped Tibs. H.C. said, "Or is it fungi tonight, eh?"

"I thought I'd have what the rest of you are eating tonight, sir."

"You disappoint me," said H.C. "Didn't you manage to catch a mouse or two, or a lizard or so as you came up, eh?"

He went off smirking. Tibs was furious.

On the further side of the ravine the ground was studded with low, stunted hawthorn trees and amongst these a cuckoo was calling. "That bird shall end up as my dinner tonight, or my name isn't Tybault Brightstone," growled Tibs. "I'll teach that idiotic old Catterwaul to laugh at me!"

And he left the camp, crossed the ravine and began stalking his way towards the hawthorns.

The cuckoo was making a great deal of noise but proved most difficult to locate. Now the bird seemed to call from this tree; now from that. The trees were clotted white with blossom, the evening air was heavy with their scent. Beneath the trees grew blue-bells, also in full flower. Tibs stalked from tree to tree, using the utmost care, creeping flat on his tummy, using the blue-bells for cover. The light was fading, the setting sun turned all the high peaks a rosy colour, the shadows in the valleys thickened. The cuckoo and Tibs played hide-and-seek; Tibs in an awful temper. Finally he glimpsed the bird flitting from one tree to another; Tibs launched himself at it in desperation and, of course, missed. He landed heavily back amongst the blue-bells. The cuckoo shouted mockingly and flew away. Tibs heard a lot of sniggering; he looked round and found Oliver peeping from behind a tree, killing himself laughing.

"Cuckoo for nicens din-dins tonight?" said Oliver.

"Shurrup!" snarled Tibs.

"Maybe just nicens munchy moss for din-dins den?" giggled Oliver.

"If you don't pipe down I'll knock your silly young block off."

Oliver came out from behind the tree. "Oh, I say. Don't take it out on me. I'm your friend."

"Some friend. I don't like being laughed at." Tibs sat down to get his breath back. "What silly birds cuckoos are," he said pettishly.

"Jolly sensible bird to get away from such an unhealthy spot," said Oliver. "Let's see what else you can find to eat. Blue-bells?"

"Oh do be quiet."

"They always look very nice and juicy to me."

"They taste vile."

"How odd. For they smell heavenly." Oliver lay down amongst the blue-bells and sniffed. "Oh I say, here's a butterfly, fast asleep."

"Well I'm not going to get tickles in my throat swallowing butterflies, thank you."

"I wasn't suggesting anything so low."

"Wake him up and ask him for the weather-forecast. Butterflies always know the weather-forecast."

Oliver put his face near the butterfly, a greenish-white one who was clinging, sound asleep, to the head of a blue-bell. "Is it going to rain?" whispered Oliver.

No reply came. Oliver put his face closer and whispered a little more loudly, "Hey, wake up. Is it going to rain?"

He paused, waiting, listening.

"Try him again. Shout," said Tibs.

Oliver put his face very near the butterfly indeed and bellowed, "Hey you, IS IT GOING TO RAIN?"

The butterfly, without opening its eyes, twiddled its legs furiously and bawled back in a voice that shook the blue-bell; "D'you want to buy a battleship?"

"Blimey!" said Oliver, rubbing his ear.

"They have fantastic loud voices on 'em," said Tibs. "They rarely speak, butterflies, but when they do it's mighty."

"You could have warned me. I'll be deaf for life."

"It simply doesn't make sense; d'you want to buy a battleship?"

"He's talking in his sleep. His eyes are shut."

"That definitely means bad weather. They always go right off when the weather turns for the worse; fall asleep and stay asleep till it sets in fair again."

"The weather looks perfectly good to me," said Oliver, gazing up at the clear sky and the sunset-rosy peaks. "Red night, shepherd's delight."

"Rot," boomed the butterfly.

"Why d'you say that?" mewed Tibs, bouncing through the blue-bells to get into the conversation.

"Storms, snow, blizzards!" shouted the butterfly.

"Couldn't make it plainer than that," said Tibs.

"Ask him about the apple-dumplings," said Oliver.

"Apple-dumplings?"

"Yes, you know. Without any flour."

"Don't be childish!" roared the butterfly, still with its eyes tight shut.

"They really are ridiculous creatures," said Tibs.

"Oh, let's leave the insect."

They walked off. The butterfly remained clinging to the blue-bell, snoring a little. It sounded like a far distant train.

"When butterflies snore loudly, human beings, who know nothing about everything, often mistake the sound for thunder," remarked Tibs. "A really very loud explosion, one of those odd sudden ones, you know, and some tom-fool of a human looks up and says it's jet breaking through the sound barrier when, more often than not, it's nothing of the sort, it's a butterfly sneezing."

"Miracles of modern science explained," said Oliver.

They descended into the ravine, back towards the camp. Twists of smoke rose in all directions from the porters' fires. Tibs said, "If H.C. starts laughing at me again, joking about fungi or edible moss or bracken shoots . . ."

"I'll tell him you've just caught and eaten a golden-eagle."

Suddenly they came upon Whiskey, Wee Hamish, Sankey and Moody deep in conversation. They were passing a bottle one to the other, taking good strong pulls at it. When they saw the two cats they stopped talking for a moment, then Hamish said, as if they had been discussing it all the time, "Jings, ye canna beat the Cairns when they're on form. They're the best team in the country."

Whiskey, who had been about to put the bottle to his lips, quickly poured a little of its contents into his right paw and began ostentatiously rubbing his left hind leg with it.

Sankey and Moody politely saluted Oliver and Tibs. "Evening, sirs."

"Evening, gentlemen. A fine night," said Hamish.

"Grand," replied Tibs heartily.

"Fabulous," said Oliver.

The two cats then passed on down the ravine. Once out of ear-shot Oliver said, "I bet they weren't talking football when we first came upon 'em."

"I bet not. And d'you notice the way old Whiskey Bylines was about to drink out of that bottle and then started rubbing himself with the stuff instead?"

"Yes, I noticed that. A strange thing to do with catnip. For it was catnip. I smelt it."

"Rum," said Tibs.

"I definitely smelt catnip, not rum."

"Chump. I mean it was a rum way to behave with a bottle of catnip."

"Odd little set-up altogether," said Oliver. "What's he doing in cahoots with those three terriers?"

The rest of the evening passed uneventfully; everyone felt

weary after the long day's march and nobody was late in getting to bed. The rabbits squirmed into their little tents, the cats snuggled into their luxurious high-altitude sleeping-bags inside their windproof tents, while the terriers, not bothering either with sleeping-bags or tents, simply curled themselves up in the lee of the large boulders strewing the mountainside and went peacefully to sleep.

Oliver, during the night, had an odd experience however; he woke suddenly to hear high-pitched barking, a wild and mocking "yappity, yap, yap," a sharp sound which seemed to come from high up the mountain-side. It didn't sound like the voice of one of the terriers. Yet, if not a terrier yapping out there, who was it? Oliver was too sleepy to ponder the problem for long.

Next day dawned fine again; the Expedition was awake shortly after sunrise. The climbing-cats set out early, with the terriers, as on the previous day; Tibs, Tom, Whiskey and the porters followed later. The track up the ravine became much steeper, more difficult and dangerous as the day wore on; the rabbits began to grumble very much. Diggory and Burrows had great trouble in getting them to carry on. The rabbits threatened to strike and down loads unless they were promised danger-money; one of them climbed on to a rock, and perching there, made a long rambling speech about what would happen to his wife and children if he returned to the valley crippled for life as a result of a mountain accident. Diggory, beneath his umbrella, listened much moved. "Aye, he's right. What will happen to his wife if he breaks a leg up here and never walks again?"

"It's a bad lookout, a bad lookout," sighed Burrows.

"And think of his children. What will become of them?" added Diggory. "Poor wee souls."

"How many children has he?" asked Tom.

"Weel, now, as a matter o' fact he has none, sir, your honour, at least none that he lets on about, for he's not a married chap, but it would be a terrible thing for his children if he had them, that's the point he's making."

"Tell that rascal if he's not down from that rock in two minutes and up the track with his load back on then he'll be rabbit-pie before he can say cow-parsley!" roared Tibs. The rabbit's speech ended abruptly.

At last, in the late afternoon, they reached Sprinkling Tarn where Base Camp was to be set up. The porters laid down their loads and set about helping the terriers to put up the tents and arrange all the equipment and climbing-gear in orderly piles, under Tom's direction. The climbers' tents were arranged in a semicircle round the big mess-tent; in the centre of the camp a flag-staff was erected and the flag of the Cat's Kingdom was run up, while the entire company cheered. Supper was then prepared; the rabbits, who were due next day to return to the lowlands; asked for permission to hold a jamboree. H.C. agreed; soon the rabbits had a huge fire burning and were crowded round it playing their accordions, mouth-organs and straw-whistles, clog-dancing, singing their beloved Border ballads, clapping, squealing and stamping, and in general having a fine, rowdy time.

Terriers and cats gathered to watch and to join in the choruses. Everyone became excited by the leaping fire, the wild shadows, the music, the squeals and shouting, the rhythmic clapping of paws and thumping of feet. Wee Hamish fetched his bagpipes and began to parade, half dancing, half marching, up and down in the firelight, playing *The Gay Gordons* and a pibroch he had composed himself, *Wee Hamish is Awa'*. The terriers cheered him frenziedly.

Because of the noise nobody at first noticed that, in a dark part of the camp, beyond the firelight, there was a whale of a battle going on. But at last the fearful yowling, howling, barking, spitting, shrieking, snapping, and growling of a first-class cat-and-dog fight rose in a great crescendo above the din of the jamboree, and everyone looked round to see a huge Manx cat spinning round and round in a mad catherine-wheel of claws and teeth and flying fur; it was Manx Scoop mixing it, furiously, with how many terriers at

once you couldn't count. Hanging on to Manx's breeches'
seat like a sort of fur-tassel fastened to a humming-top was
Ranjit Singh the mongoose. He was whistling shrilly all the
time through his clenched teeth, like a kettle on the boil.
Altogether it was a fight well worth attention.

CHAPTER FIVE

CHAMPAGNE AND ATTACK

For a few moments everyone simply stood watching; too astonished to move. Then Wee Hamish flung down his bagpipes, uttered a wild cry and hurled himself into the fight. The rest of the terriers, seeing their hero, Wee Hamish, taking part in the fray, hung back for only a second or so, then flew forward to fight too. The climbing-cats tried to break up the battle. Meantime Manx Scoop spun round and round in a series of cataclysmic somersaults, clawing and biting as he spun, the terriers whirled round him, the cats whirled round the terriers and the mongoose, teeth dug deep into Manx, was flourished in airy circles, faster and faster, like a crazy fly-whisk.

The rabbits, after staring, frozen with horror, scuttled off and hid in their little tents.

The uproar of the fighting echoed and re-echoed amongst the mountains encircling the tarn. At last, from the thick of the rumpus, there emerged the figures of two cats pawing and hugging one another, while the mongoose, still whistling furiously, clung to the seat of one of them. They were H.C. and Manx Scoop. The rest of the cats and terriers seethed round them; nobody could say for certain whether H.C. and Manx were fighting or embracing. But at last it was possible to hear something of what they were shouting at each other.

"My dear Scoop! Fancy finding you here! What a simply splendid thing! How did you get here? How absolutely lovely!" boomed H.C. over and over again. Meantime Manx Scoop was yowling.

"Blasted terriers! Mad dogs! Where's that doctor? H.C.,

for the love of Moses get me a shot of anti-rabies serum!"

"My dear Manx Scoop, my dear Manx Scoop, fancy meeting you here!"

"Mad dog, mad dog, get him off me!" bellowed Manx, dancing about in pain and pawing imploringly at H.C.

"Your trouble, Mr. Scoop, is that you're wearing a mongoose," said Scratch, politely.

"Mongoose!" roared Manx. "So that's where he's got to, is it? I'll give him mongoose! Get him off! Prise him loose!"

Scratch gingerly tried to remove the mongoose from Manx's seat.

"He won't leave go, sir!"

"But great Lucifer, I can't, I *won't* spend the rest of my life . . .!"

"We must have a drink on this, we really must!" crooned H.C. "What a lovely meeting! Where's the honeydew-champagne, Felix?"

"That was for when we made the summit, sir"

"Nonsense; champagne here and now. I insist. It isn't every day that I bump into one of my oldest and dearest friends at the foot of the H.K.P."

"To hell with champagne," shouted poor Manx. "Save me from this mongoose!"

"He simply won't leave go!" gasped Scratch, tugging hard at the mongoose. Manx roared louder and leapt in the air higher than ever.

"Keep still, keep still, Manx. I see what's the matter now, dashed mongoose has got his teeth into you," said H.C., as if making a brilliant discovery. "Let me have a word with him. Just stand still," he added.

Manx, wincing with pain, did his best to stand still. H.C. bent towards the mongoose, who hung like grim death on to Manx, his eyes tight shut.

All the other animals gathered round to watch this drama between Sir Hywel Catterwaul, Manx Scoop and the mongoose.

"It's Ranjit Singh, isn't it?" asked H.C., inspecting the

mongoose and then glancing up at Manx, who nodded grimly. "Aha, I thought it was. Splendid little chap, spunky as they come. I remember him well. Glad to see he's still with you, Manx."

"You're joking, surely," murmured Manx. H.C. didn't hear this one; he was bending close towards the mongoose again. Then once more he glanced up at Manx. "Interestin' how they always shut their eyes once they've got a death-grip on their opponent, isn't it? Obviously he thinks you're a cobra. I once recall seein' a fight between a cobra and a mongoose when I was on leave, fishin' holiday y'know, mahseer, in a spot somewhere between Dabidhura and Dhunaghat, or was it Champawat or Chowgarh?"

"Why not write it up for the Zoological Society, H.C.? They'd love it. And you could send 'em a chewed portion of my person as a specimen, if there's any left of me by that time," said Manx grimly. H.C. began roaring with laughter.

"My dear feller, you always did have a lovely sense of humour!" H.C. drew a long sigh, wiped his eyes, then bent down towards the mongoose and spoke a few curt words to him in Urdu. The mongoose at once let go of Manx, dropped to his feet, opened his eyes, stood smartly to attention, and saluted. "Sahib!"

"Had your master been a snake, Ranjit Singh, you would deserve the highest praise," said H.C. "As it is . . ."

"As it is, Ranjit Singh, you fool, I shall never be able to sit down in comfort again!" roared Manx, shaking his fist at the mongoose, who thereupon gave another smart salute and repeated, "Sahib!"

"In future, you steaming Tishbite, when you fix your teeth into somebody, make sure it's not me!"

"Sahib, I absolutely consider myself most unfortunate, for I see that a very grave confusion arose. But indeed, sahib, when these wild creatures attacked I was greatly dismayed; however immediately I recovered my scattered senses I seized the largest of the enemy without hesitation. It was indeed a misfortune, sahib, that in point of fact this large individual was yourself."

"Next time there's any kind of a fight on, Ranjit Singh, I must forbid you to take any part in it. Without your gallant assistance I should be in much better shape than I now find myself."

"Champagne, where's that champagne?" boomed H.C. "I insist upon champagne to drink the very good health of my dear old fellow *shikar*, Manx Scoop!"

"Better fetch out the bubbly, Felix," said Scratch, "We'll celebrate the H.K.P. in Worcester Sauce."

Felix sighed and went to fetch the champagne. H.C. seated himself on a patch of turf in the firelight.

"And now, m'dear feller," he said to Manx, "let's hear what you're up to in these parts. Huntin', shootin', fishin', or just plain stirrin' the place up in general, as O. Slim-Bones would have said, eh, what?"

"O. Slim-Bones, what a glorious type he must have been!" said Manx, sitting down very carefully beside H.C. "I was giving an after-dinner speech at the Explorers' Club the other night, and I told 'em that story of Slim-Bones and the mouse-trap. It brought the house down. Hope you don't mind me borrowing one of your Slim-Bones stories, but they are so very good!"

"Slim-Bones, like all great cats throughout the course of history, belongs to everyone," said H.C. "And it's a sign of your own great spirit, Manx, that you can so thoroughly grasp the greatness of O. Slim-Bones. Not like some miserable cats, mis-er-able CATS!" repeated H.C. with a growl, "who have never even heard of him!"

"What, never heard of O. Slim-Bones! Must be clots," said Manx.

"Mind you, not everyone approved of him at the time! Oh, far from it!" said H.C. with a chuckle. "A lot of the older johnnies took a very dim view of O.S.B.; thought him a wild young chap, not at all the sort they liked to see in the Alpine Club."

"Really," said Manx. "Don't suppose it worried him,

though. Mind if I lie on my front?" He rolled over on to his tummy, a trifle stiffly. "Take me a day or two to get over that mauling," he added.

"How come you got mixed up in such a fantastic fight?" asked Scratch.

Manx said, "That's what I'd like to know."

"Yes, how did it happen?" said H.C. "So exactly like you to appear out of the blue in the thick of a battle-royal that I never gave it a thought, just took it for granted you would roar out of the night fighting every damn terrier in the territory, but come to think of it, how *did* it happen?"

"Ask me," said Manx. "All I know for certain is that I was ambushed."

"Who by?"

"That I don't know. I was camping by Sty Head Tarn, my tents and porters are still there, and I'd gone up on to Esk Hause to take a look at that big rock-face up there, Great End I think they call it. I left it rather late coming down, getting a bit dusky; I was just starting back to camp when these two terriers jumped me from behind a rock. I had three rabbits with me, but of course they fled at once. Fortunately Ranjit Singh was not far away. Let's correct that remark; unfortunately, for my posterior, Ranjit wasn't far away and he at once came running. Well, we fought all over the place, those two terriers and I; matter of fact I was under the impression there were three of 'em, one hanging on to my seat and the other two attacking me from the front, but the third was that darn imbecile, my faithful mongoose. Anyway, to cut a painful story short, we rolled a long way downhill fighting furiously, and just as I thought I was getting the best of it the whole darn landscape rose up in arms. And then you were suddenly hanging round my neck, shouting for champagne."

"Where *is* it?" roared H.C. Tibs sang out, "Champagne coming up now, sir!"

"High time, too," said H.C.

"Who were the two terriers who attacked you, Mr.

Scoop?" asked Oliver. "Could you describe them?"

"I didn't see 'em all that well, what with the fading light and the fact they took me by surprise; they were small, very hairy chaps. But that doesn't help much. They are none of 'em very big, and all pretty hairy."

"None of this lot here?" asked H.C.

Manx looked round. "No, can't see 'em amongst this bunch. They must have cleared off when we stopped fighting."

Oliver looked round at the terriers; all were present except Sankey and Moody.

"Didn't imagine any of our terriers would be responsible," said H.C. "This Expedition has enough on its plate without trying to kidnap Manx Scoop into the bargain!"

"There are some who might prefer me out of the way," said Manx lightly.

H.C. started laughing. "Take that as read. Always have been, always will be, plenty of people who prefer you out of the way, Manx, eh, what! But that doesn't answer my original question; what brings you to this part of the world in the first place?"

Manx paused a moment, then grinned wickedly. "Well, to tell you the truth, H.C., and you are far too old and valued a friend for me to tell anything but the truth, I'm here to scoop Whiskey Bylines over the story of the ascent of the H.K.P."

"Whiskey Bylines? Never heard of him. Who is he?" said H.C.

"Special correspondent from the *Cat's Courier* with, I understand, exclusive rights to the story of this Expedition."

"Oh, that fat, silly black-and-white feller? Had never heard of O. Slim-Bones!"

"He's fat, yes, and black-and-white, yes, and some, no doubt, would say silly. If he has never heard of O. Slim-Bones he must be pretty dim."

"Shouldn't be difficult to scoop him, Manx," said H.C. "For one thing you'll get much further up the mountain than he ever will, he's too dashed fat to climb. And anyway, I'll keep you in touch with everything that's going on, my dear chap, rest assured of that."

"Awfully nice of you, H.C."

Whiskey, in the background, had been straining his ears to catch this conversation. Now he gasped, appalled.

"But, Sir Hywel! You simply can't do this! The *Courier* has bought the sole rights of the story of this Expedition!"

"The *Courier*," snapped H.C., "has not bought the sole rights of *my* story of the H.K.P."

"You are part of the Expedition, Sir Hywel."

"My story is my own story, and if I want to sit down in the evenings in my tent and talk over my part in the day's events with my dear old friend, Manx Scoop, nothing can stop me," said H.C.

"This is most unfair, Sir Hywel, most unfair," said Whiskey, very put out.

"I'll have a quiet word with the old boy later; get him to see sweet reason," Felix muttered to Whiskey.

The champagne was now opened with a pleasant popping of corks, glasses were filled and handed round. Whiskey excused himself saying he didn't feel very well; he went to his tent, took a bottle labelled *Hair Restorer* from his First Aid chest and sat moodily drinking that.

H.C., armed with a glass of champagne, stood up and raised it high above his head. "To my old friend, Manx Scoop, and the pleasure of meeting him at the start of our great adventure on the H.K.P. May we all reach the top together!"

"To Manx Scoop!" mewed and yapped the other animals.

The toast was drunk; Manx Scoop bowed to the company. "Thank you, gentlemen. May we have some truly great days ahead of us."

The evening was a merry one after that. H.C. wanted Manx Scoop to strike his camp at Sty Head Tarn and join the Expedition, but Manx said he thought it would be best if he remained a solo unit on the mountain, although naturally, a friendly one. "What I mean is, it wouldn't be ethics for me to move in to your camp lock, stock and barrel, though there's absolutely nothing to prevent me dropping in from time to time for a drink, or your chaps calling on me."

"What happens if another attempt is made to ambush you?" asked Oliver.

"I can't see that happening," said Manx. "I'm not the sort to be caught napping twice. However, in case any unfriendly fellows are waiting for me at Sty Head when I get back there tonight, or tomorrow morning as it will now more likely be, may I borrow a couple or so of your terriers, H.C.? I'll return 'em to you tomorrow."

"Of course!" said H.C. "But if you do have any more trouble, woe betide the terriers of this part of the world! I'll send a personal telegram to the Queen, telling her that the natives of this District are hostile, and we'll have a battalion of the Royal Cat Light Infantry up here in no time. And that won't be pleasant for any trouble-making terriers, oh no! Eh, what?"

"That'll no be necessary, sir," said Wee Hamish. "There's no terriers in these parts will be ready to so much as bear a bristle at Mr. Scoop now that they realize he's a friend of yours, Sir Hywel."

"I'm delighted to hear it," said old H.C. drily.

"Oliver and I will come with you too, Manx, when you go," said Tibs. "There are some rocks at Sty Head that I want to look at, and young Oliver here will enjoy the walk."

It was not until well after midnight that the party set out; Manx, Tibs, Oliver, Wee Hamish and Rabsie. They carried hurricane-lamps; the two terriers were armed with dirks, Tibs had his geologist's hammer held at the ready, while H.C. had insisted upon Manx taking an old army revolver with him.

The party picked their way down the rough, steep track of Esk Hause, towards Sty Head, their hurricane-lamps casting swinging patches of light upon the black boulders and giant slabs of rock-face bordering the route, while the mountains brooded in the dark and the stars, bright and huge, trembled like great drops of dew hung on high branches of the night.

"Won't be all that long till sunrise, now," said Manx.

"Aye," said Wee Hamish, "you can smell the morn coming. It'll be another fine day, but there's rain on the way at the back of it."

Suddenly a sharp yapping rang out of the darkness on their left. "Hsst, sahib," whispered Ranjit Singh, "the devils come again!"

"Not this time," said Manx, after a moment of listening. "No terrier, that one. That was a fox. I heard one last night, too."

"So did I," said Oliver, who had recognized the high-pitched yappity-yap-yap as the sound that had woken him in his tent down in Grain Gill.

"There'll be no more attacks on you by terriers, Mr. Scoop, I can vouch for that," said Wee Hamish. "I'll see word gets round that you're a friend of the owd Brigadier."

"There should never have been any attack on Manx Scoop in the first place, Hamish," said Tibs severely.

"Och, weel," said Hamish, with a slight cough, "it was a misunderstanding, ye ken. These things will happen, Mr. Brightstone. We all bite the wrong cat, or dog, as the case may be, sometimes. Even Ranjit Singh here has been known to do it. And Mr. Scoop was pointed out as a person the Expedition needed to be rid of. Get him off the mountain, we terriers were told."

"I'd love to know who told you that," said Tibs.

"It doesn't matter," said Manx, cheerfully. "And it was a good fight while it lasted."

"Aye, it was that," said Hamish and Rabsie together, happily. "And an even better one for the lads who jumped ye in the furst place, Mr. Scoop," added Hamish.

"I hope so," said Manx. "I did my best to make it a truly good fight."

"Ye had two bonny lads agin ye," said Hamish.

"It felt that way," said Manx. "I'd like to meet 'em again

some time, under more friendly circumstances."

"There's no tellin' you won't," said Rabsie, cheerfully.

When they reached the tarn where Manx Scoop's tents were pitched the clouds had collected low there, as they do before dawn, and lay like a thick mist. No sound came from the camp as the party drew near. Wee Hamish whispered, "Stay here; I'll go ahead; if the terriers or anyone else for that matter are waitin' to surprise ye, I'll gie them a guid wee flea in the ear." He crept forward into the mist; the others waited behind a large pile of stones. An eerie little wind blew over the high open ground on the top of the pass; tiny waves lapped across the surface of the tarn and slapped the shore with small, soft hands. At this hour, in the dark and the mist, Sty Head was one of the lonely lost places of the world.

Presently Hamish came creeping back. "Mr. Scoop."

"Yes?"

"The camp is empty."

"What about the rabbits?"

"There's nae a rabbit, nor any living soul in sight. It's a' quiet and empty as the grave."

"That's rum," said Manx.

They all went down to the camp. It was, as Hamish had said, deserted. Manx looked round carefully. He found that nothing was missing except some potted frogs' legs. And, of coarse, the rabbits.

"Let's brew some coffee and think a bit," said Manx.

The mongoose quickly had coffee served; they sat on the verge of the tarn, round a small fire, sipping the coffee while the daylight seeped through the mist, which curled into long streamers that blew upwards to coil round the mountain tops, or spread into broad white cushion-shapes which floated slowly down the Pass like a shoal of lazy white whales. Soon the tarn lay clear and fair within its green surround of turf, the mountains shining above it, the blue sky shining above them.

When every trace of night and mist had gone, but not

until then, the cats and the terriers seated in the camp saw three terrified-looking rabbits crawl out from under a rock some little way up the mountainside. They came timidly stealing towards the tents, stopping every other minute to move their long ears, listening, their whiskers and noses twitching rapidly. When they saw Manx and his companions drinking coffee they broke into a fast scuttle and in a minute or two were pouring out a breathless tale to Manx.

"Foxes, your honour, hundreds of foxes, broke into the tents, carried our poor lads off kicking and screaming; only by a mercy we hid in time; it was all over in a flash!"

"Which way did they go?"

"We never saw, your honour, it was so dark, and we stayed hid, your honour. We were that afeared."

Manx looked round the steep mountainsides, the wild crags scarred with deep black gullies, the long red scree-beds, the distant heights of rock on which patches of snow still sparkled. It was a savage place, fit for savage happenings.

"D'ye think they'll have ate them, yer honour?" stammered one of the rabbits.

Manx shook his head. "It's a bad business."

"There's two foxes now, seesta!" squealed another rabbit in terror.

"Where?" said Manx, quickly. "Get me my rifle, Ranjit." To the rabbit again, "Where?"

"Up there, on yon crag, seesta!"

They all looked up to where the rabbit pointed with a shaking paw. Two grey, hairy, tough little figures were skipping down the crags. "They're no foxes," said Hamish.

"Nay," said Rabsie, "it's Sankey and Moody."

Hamish put his paws to his mouth and uttered a long, ringing halloo. One of the terriers barked in reply.

Then they came leaping, bounding and bouncing down the mountainside to the camp.

"Seen any foxes?" called Hamish, as they ran nearer.

"Aye."

"Which way?"

"Up yon gill!"

Sankey and Moody rushed into the camp. "They went up yon great gill, into the mountain. Seven rabbits they had with 'em, prisoners like. We watched 'em go. It was too dark to count how many foxes, but it were too many for us to tackle alone, like, so we let 'em go."

"We'd best get back to Base Camp and warn H.C.," said Tibs. "Manx, we can't leave you here alone with three rabbits and one mongoose."

Ranjit Singh drew himself up, his eyes went red as fire and he spat, rather than said, "Sahib, are you mistaking me for a creature no better than a rabbit?"

"Good gracious no, Ranjit Singh!" said Tibs hastily, scared by the furious look of the mongoose. "But against so many foxes what could even two great warriors like you and your master do?"

"We could do plenty," said Ranjit Singh, showing all his very many, very white, very sharp teeth.

"I shall stay here," said Manx, "with Ranjit Singh and these three poor rabbits, but if I may I'll keep Sankey and Moody, too. That makes one mongoose, two terriers and one Manx Scoop against, well, several foxes. But we four are all able to fight well, as we proved to one another last night; and if the foxes attack and there are too many for us I'll fire H.C.'s revolver three times, fast in succession, then one last shot a little afterwards, and that will mean we need reinforcements."

So it was agreed. Tibs, Oliver, Hamish and Rabsie returned to Base Camp, keeping a sharp watch for any sign of foxes, but seeing none. Manx, Ranjit Singh, Sankey and Moody, left at Sty Head Tarn with the three rabbits, set about gathering stones and building a parapet round the sides of the camp facing the mountain; on the forth side they were protected by the tarn. Then they built a fortified look-out tower on top of a nearby rock and stationed two of the rabbits in it. "We'll keep a constant watch, all round the clock," said Manx. "Being prepared for attack always goes at least half-way towards preventing it."

"D'you think they'll have ate yon poor lads?" the rabbits kept asking Manx. He said, "I don't know. They might keep 'em alive as hostages. Might not. Might eat 'em, might not. Who can say? But one thing I promise you, I'll do everything I can to find out what has happened to them, and if possible, to save them."

CHAPTER SIX

OLD LEADER, NEW LEADER

H.C. WAS VERY annoyed to hear about the foxes. "What a blitherin' nuisance! We could have done without a parcel of troublesome foxes! After the rabbits, were they? Well, let's get rid of all our darn rabbits, then perhaps the foxes won't be interested in us."

The rabbit porters were due to be paid off and sent home anyway. They could go no higher; now the terriers would take over as porters.

The rabbits lined up in the sunshine waiting to receive their wages, only too delighted to think that they were going to get away from these hated high regions.

Besides being paid their wages, each was presented with a small silk Expedition flag as a souvenir. They gave the Expedition leaders a rousing final cheer and then away they all ran, going back down Grain Gill a lot faster than they had come up.

Whiskey Bylines went with them. For one thing his porters refused to stay any longer in the high mountains once the other rabbits had left and in the second place Whiskey was completely disgusted with H.C.; poor Whiskey said that he had never heard of a special correspondent being given such unfair treatment in all his life and he was going back to Seathwaite to cable the *Courier* about it.

So his porters struck his tent and away went Whiskey. He left behind him, half concealed in a crack between two boulders, three empty bottles labelled, *Embrocation, Hair Restorer* and *Sun Tan Oil*. But they all smelled of catnip.

The cats and terriers now turned to the great *massif* of the

H.K.P. Their immediate objective was to establish Camp One at the foot of the first of the five peaks that made up the mountain; this peak they had already named Catterwaul Pike.

Tibs was to remain at Base Camp to do some geological work on samples of mud taken from Sprinkling Tarn. Tom Black was also to remain at Base Camp as anchor man. Titch and Tiny were to stay there as guard dogs, Yorky Boy and Pooks as general assistants to Tibs and Tom.

The other animals set out to make Camp One. They were to keep in touch with Base Camp by radio.

The weather was hotter than ever, but with a threat of a storm. The sky became so pallid with heat that it seemed almost white; the mountains sank into the heat haze. The cats' route lay over a never ending landscape of huge boulders, a jumbled sea of sun-quaking stone. It was like climbing in the proverbial oven.

At noon an odd little breeze suddenly arrived, a welcome relief at first, darting and fluttering and leaping, cool and encouraging. But gradually it grew stronger, whipping round them in gusts. Faint rumblings could be heard in the far distance, coming out of the blanket of heat-haze. "Is that thunder, or a butterfly snoring?" murmured Oliver.

And now the cats had reached a very bad place in their ascent; the route was barred by a huge wall of rock; the only possible way up it was by a slit of narrow, dark chimney which dwindled away, on the upper pitches, into nothing but a crack.

The cats studied the rock, discussing what was best to be done. Fixed-ropes would have to be fastened across it for the terriers. Scratch and Oliver started up first; they climbed the chimney pretty quickly, but when they reached the crack things became very much more difficult. Felix and Hamish climbed up the chimney and joined Scratch and Oliver upon a big boulder which, wedged across the top of the chimney, made a useful resting place. Hamish, upon reaching this chock-stone, became very excited at finding himself so high, and began barking loudly. Felix was furious with him. "Stop barking this instant, or I'll send you back to Base Camp!" Hamish stopped barking and wagged his tail. "No hard feelings?" he said, cheerily.

Scratch and Oliver were busy examining the crack. H.C., a long way below, stood staring up, watching them. "Will it go?" he shouted. Scratch shouted back, "I think so!" Soon he and Oliver started up the crack, Scratch leading; Felix and Hamish belayed them with ropes. Scratch could be heard going slowly up the crack. "It's a real rat of a thing, this one!" he called down to Oliver, Felix and Hamish. Hamish, always keen to help, yapped back, "Shall I play a wee pibroch to help ye up?"

"No!" snarled Scratch.

It was not until late afternoon that the ropes were all fixed ready for the terriers. By this time the sky had grown very dark and the horizon was purple with the coming storm. A decision now had to be made; whether to leave getting the terriers up the rock-face until the morrow, or whether to try to get them up before the storm broke. Scratch thought they should wait until next day; but H.C., asked for his opinion, gave his usual reply, "My instincts tell me to carry on up."

So the terriers started up the climb, the ascent now made much easier by the fixed-ropes. The little dogs got up very well, being wonderfully tough and agile. Lastly came H.C.

All the time that the terriers had been climbing, the sky had been growing darker, the wind stronger and the thunder nearer. Lightning flickered. As Scratch, Oliver and Felix hurried to get the last of the terriers off the face a peal of thunder crashed immediately overhead and a sheet of lightning danced over the rocks. Oliver called down to H.C., "Stop when you reach the chock-stone, sir! Don't try coming up the crack in this!"

The air was solid with rain which, upon striking the

ground, at once exploded into shooting jets of water. The thunder roared and boomed, the lightning ripped over the mountain with blinding brilliance. From below came snatches of H.C.'s unmistakable catterwaul. "Up! Up! Up!"

"Ye gods, he's going to come up the crack! In this!" gasped Felix.

"Stay where you are!" roared Scratch to the old cat far below.

"Coming up!" yowled H.C. He raised his face to them and they could see his angry eyes and bristling whiskers; the sight frightened Felix. "There's no stopping him!" he wailed.

"Silly old haddock!" stormed Scratch, grinding his teeth in rage. "I'll give him up, up, up; he's got a mania for up. It'll be down, down for him if he doesn't watch out."

"Coming up!" yowled H.C. once more. His voice got lost in the thunder.

"O.K. come on up then!" screeched Scratch. "Let's all go mad!"

"Oh my sainted Aunt Fitchit, if this isn't asking for trouble I don't know what is! The lightning will strike him, you wait," moaned Felix.

"Go up in fire and brimstone like Beelzebub," said Scratch. "What the silly old geezer deserves, and all."

"It isn't funny," said Felix, cowering amongst the rocks. "I'm soaked to the skin and the electricity in the atmosphere will . . ." His words were cut short by a great earth-and-sky quake of thunder, a blue wave of lightning scoured the rocks, there was a fearful shriek from H.C., the rope between him and Scratch went taut and a horrid smell of singed fur reached their noses.

"I daren't look, I daren't look!" wailed Felix.

There was dead silence now for a moment. Scratch at last summoned the nerve to look. H.C. had come off the crack and was dangling, motionless, at the end of the rope, puffs of smoke were coming from his tail.

"Blimey!" said Scratch.

"He's on fire!" cried Felix, peering down at H.C. too.

"The rain will put him out," said Scratch unkindly, between his teeth.

After a fearful tussle the three cats got H.C.'s dangling body on to the chock-stone in the chimney. Here the old cat regained consciousness; he opened his eyes and blinked. "Up, up!" he exclaimed feebly. "Nobody shall stop me. Up, I say!" He sank back with a groan. Felix said, "Take it easy, H.C. You came off."

"Something's burnin'," said H.C. "Don't waste time fussin' over me. Send for the fire-brigade."

"It's your tail, sir. You got a bit singed. The lightning caught you."

"Did it, by gad? Wondered what had happened," said H.C. "Never been struck by lightnin' before. Quite an experience, eh, what?"

While they waited for the storm to die down the cats discussed what they should do. H.C. was clearly a stretcher-case. There was a stretcher amongst the gear at the top of the rock-face; Scratch climbed up and fetched it and two terriers to assist as stretcher-bearers. Alec and Brat Wilson were chosen for this task. The other terriers were left under the leadership of Wee Hamish to pitch tents for Camp One and guard the camp until the cats returned.

Carrying H.C. back to Base Camp proved a nightmare journey. The rocks were very slippery and it grew dark quickly. The two terriers, Scratch and Felix took turns carrying the stretcher in pairs, Oliver acted as guide. It was very late when they stumbled into Base Camp. Tom and Tibs were asleep; the barking of the dogs roused them. Tibs brewed tea while Tom gave H.C. treatment. The old cat had a torn ligament in his paw, concussion, badly bruised ribs and a big burned patch on his tail. He would have to stay at Base Camp until he could limp on three legs and then go by easy stages down to Seathwaite to recuperate.

H.C., still very dazed, was furious to find himself lying in a tent back at Base Camp, listening to talk about sending him down to Seathwaite.

"Rats, rot, rubbish!" he snapped. "Be back on my paws in no time. Up, let me keep up."

" 'Fraid not, H.C.," said Tom. "It's rotten luck, really hard lines, but you must face the fact that you've got some quite nasty injuries."

H.C. continued to argue; Tom fetched a tablet to quieten him down. H.C. refused to take it.

"Dash it, I don't like pills. Namby-pamby things. Give me a good dose of Gregory Powder, if you must give me something, and leave me to it."

"Gregory Powder!" gasped the affronted Tom. "This isn't the Dark Ages!"

"Better than these new-fangled drugs you young chaps pin your faith in."

"Come on, H.C.," said Oliver coaxingly. "Swallow that pill. Tom knows what he's up to."

"But what will it do to me?" asked H.C. eyeing the pill warily.

"Make you have a nice little nap," said Oliver.

"But drat it, I don't want a nap! I feel perfectly wide awake and fit as they come."

"You've had a very nasty knock on the head, H.C.," said Felix.

"And will be landing another, pronto, if you carry on like this," growled Scratch under his breath. "We can't spend all night chuntering about a blooming pill."

"Come on, H.C." begged Felix.

Oliver stole out of the tent, leaving the others to argue with H.C. When he came back he was carrying a saucer of tea and a piece of cheese. "Have a small snack, H.C.," he said encouragingly.

"That's the first intelligent suggestion I've heard for a long time," said H.C. He began lapping the tea noisily. Oliver fiddled about with the cheese, then handed it to H.C. who inspected it. "Cheese late at night. H'm."

"The protein content will pick you up, sir," said Oliver. "And you know how you do like cheese, sir."

"Oh, I know I like cheese, my boy, but at this hour of night cheese doesn't always like me."

"Just to please me, sir. I'm certain you'll sleep like a top. And it's only a very small piece."

The other cats, with an inkling of what was afoot, watched with encouraging smiles as H.C. ate the cheese. "There was a hard bit in the middle," he said.

"Was there, sir? How odd. Sorry about that," said Oliver.

"Shame Slim-Bones isn't here," said H.C. "He was always wonderin' what it would be like to be struck by lightnin'. Which reminds me of the story of my great-aunt Letitia and the thunder-bolt. My great-aunt was sittin' there, you know, on the hearth-rug; she was not feelin' the least nervous, though there was a very noisy storm in progress and they had put an antimacassar over the cheval-glass and hidden the scissors . . ." His head drooped sideways, he gave a jerky snore, woke up again, muttered, "Odd thing was, y'know, that she always swore that the glimpse she got of it before it exploded was *green*." And then H.C. fell sound asleep as if he had been switched off like a light.

"Whew!" said Tom. "That was clever of you, Oliver. I don't like tricking people into taking medicine, but we all need a rest, even if he doesn't."

"Him with his up, up, up," said Scratch. "I said that up, up, up, would send him down, down, and now it has."

"Like snakes and ladders," said Oliver.

"Well, we shall have to rethink what we're going to do now our Leader is out for the count," said Tom.

That was the big question indeed; who should take over as Leader? Five cats remained; Tom, Tibs, Felix, Oliver and Scratch. Oliver, obviously, was not in the running; he was too young. Tom felt that as medical officer he already had sufficient responsibility. Tibs didn't wish to be Leader; he insisted, modestly, that he hadn't the right personality. He felt that Felix, a schoolmaster, would make a good Leader.

But both Scratch and Tom, thinking of Felix's moment of panic when he had 'seen' the grinning red face, felt that Felix would not be a very sound choice. "Inclines to hysteria," thought Tom. "Panicky," reflected Scratch. Felix, a sensitive cat, guessed what they were thinking and said, "Why not choose Scratch? After all, he's the best climber amongst us, and we're here to climb a mountain, dash it all. So why not choose Scratch?"

So Scratch became Leader.

The cats then went to sleep. Next morning, early, Scratch crawled out of his tent; everything was white with snow. "Blimey, what a change!" he said.

"Who says butterflies don't know what they're talking about?" said Oliver to Tibs.

"I told you, they're always dead right on weather forecasts," replied Tibs.

"The weather's nearly always bad at this altitude," said Felix. "It's the worst obstacle we're up against, really."

"Still, you wouldn't have thought it could change that quick," said Oliver.

"Up here it can be mid-winter one day, mid-summer the next, and back again."

"So we see, curse it."

After breakfast, Scratch, Tibs, Oliver, Felix and Brat Wilson left Base Camp for Camp One. Tom remained at Base Camp with H.C. As soon as the old cat was fit enough he would go down to Seathwaite and Tom would move up to Camp One. Scratch and his climbers would meantime press on with the assault upon the H.K.P.

When the others had left, Tom went to see H.C. He had just woken up and at first couldn't think what had happened. By degrees he recalled the events of the previous day.

"By jove, I mustn't waste time lyin' here. You must get me up and about again, Tom. Onwards and upwards. Who's taken over as Leader while I'm out of the struggle?"

Tom explained that Scratch had been appointed Leader.

H.C. was appalled "That young tearaway! Why, he hasn't even got a decent hair-cut!"

And poor old H.C. lay miserably tossing and fretting. "Not even a hair-cut!"

CHAPTER SEVEN

BAGPIPES IN THE NIGHT

SCRATCH LED HIS party back to Camp One; loose-lying snow made the going difficult. The rocks were slippery and the route of yesterday hard to follow. The cats put out marker-flags; they were bright orange and had been given to the Expedition by a firm making tinned food. They read, "Cats are fit on Fitbits." Oliver amused himself by reading each flag differently as he stuck it into the snow. "Fits are fab on Catbits." "Bits are tuff on Catfits." "Kits are fat on Biftabs." The small orange flags stood lonely but brave in the snow as the climbers pressed onwards.

The clouds, grey and brooding, now smothered the tops and the cats could see little as they climbed. Certain landmarks remembered from the previous day helped them. The fixed-ropes on the rock-wall made that unpleasant place reasonably straightforward to get up. They now called it *Catterwaul's Folly*. "*Not* the official title," giggled Felix.

They reached Camp One early in the afternoon to find everything well organized by Hamish. Soon after their arrival it started to snow again and continued to do so all night. Next morning masses of snow lay everywhere, but the day itself looked clear and Scratch decided to take an advance party to establish Camp Two.

Felix was left at Camp One; he had suddenly started to compose a poem and had gone very moony in consequence. During breakfast he had put a pat of butter in his tea instead of a lump of sugar and later he was seen trying to light his pipe with a pencil-sharpener.

"He's seized up wi' inspiration. A wee Rabbie Burns," said Hamish.

"I'm not taking him with me in that state," said Scratch to Tibs. "He'll be driving a piton into my behind under the impression that I'm a bulge of rock." Tibs agreed.

Felix was not at all keen on remaining alone at Camp One.

"We'll leave you Brat Wilson. He's worth ten," said Scratch.

Brat was very put out upon hearing that he had to stay with Felix. "Yon gurning idiot," he said.

Scratch, these arrangements made, set out with Tibs, Oliver and the terriers, Hamish, Bits, Jack Russell and Rabsie, to make Camp Two.

Felix, with a sinking feeling, watched them go; a row of grinning toothy red faces flashed before his eyes and he felt a strong urge to run after his friends shouting, "Don't leave me!" But at the back of his mind words were marching and parading as they had been all morning; a new poem had him under its spell. The toothy faces faded, he went into his tent, took out a notebook, opened it and wrote:

"*To the Mountain*

The mystery is the mountain. Mountain is mystery.
Mist enshrouded, cloud-driven, rock-riven
Loud noised down winded slopes, our frozen feet
Explore with movements tentatively brutal."

There he came to a halt. He sat chewing his pencil and twiddling his whiskers. "I don't like *frozen* feet. Our questing, searching, stumbling, fumbling? No. Fearless feet? Perhaps." He leaned back and stared up into the tent roof, which was blue and created the impression of a clear, fine sky. "Our frozen feet, our *fearless* feet." This was to be a very modern poem; at least Felix hoped it was, he had an awful feeling that most of his poetry was hideously old-fashioned. "Press on, press on. Tentatively brutal. Shall we invade that lofty summit where great eagles glide?"

Brat put his head in. "What's to eat?"

"Eh?"

"Dinner."

"It's your job to get dinner, not mine. You ever seen eagles up here?"

"Nay."

"H.C. has."

"Oh aye?"

"I suppose they do come here sometimes."

"Aye."

"So if I put, 'That summit where great eagles glide' it won't be nonsense?"

"Aye."

"It will be, or it won't be nonsense?"

"We-ee-el . . ."

"There *is* such a thing as poetic licence."

"Oh aye."

"You think the line is all right otherwise?"

"Aye."

Long pause. Felix chewed his pencil, muttering to himself, his eyes closed.

> "This is the reason
> We climb, out of season,
> Where snows melt, and the,
> No, while the,
> Rose blooms in the valley gardens."

"Dash it, you can't say 'out of season'; this *is* the season for climbing these bally mountains. Out of season would be mid-winter."

Felix had forgotten that Brat was present. Brat stood watching Felix. A slight grin twitched the corners of the terrier's mouth. At last Felix opened his eyes again and saw Brat, who at once looked solemn as a judge.

"Oh, I thought you'd gone. I say, does this scan?

> This is the reason
> We climb in the season
> When snows melt
> And the rose blooms in the valley gardens.
> And the great clouds, silver-tipped
> Salute the slim-hipped moon—"

"What aye!" said Brat.

"Great clouds. I've already had great eagles. Huge clouds, maybe?" And Felix closed his eyes again and muttered, "Huge. Vast. Large. Giant." He chewed his pencil some more.

"Would tatie-pot suit?" asked Brat, at last.

"Big?"

"For two."

"What in hell are you talking about?" growled Felix, opening his eyes and glaring at Brat.

"Weel, medium-sized," said Brat.

"Oh, get out!"

"If tha' dustna fancy it, I'll eat it meself!" snarled Brat and bounced away.

"These natives!" groaned Felix. "What a load of clots! All they know about is sheep and rain, and all they can say is, 'Aye. Wee-el. Oh Aye.' What a lot! Now I've lost my train of thought, thanks to that monosyllabic mugwump."

Half an hour later the tatie-pot was simmering nicely and Brat was lying comfortably in a tent with a large sheet of paper in front of him, his pencil in his hand, his pipe in his mouth. He wrote furiously, then took his pipe from his mouth and read aloud,

> "They talk of the climbin' of Ev'rest
>   Of Hilary, Hunt and Tenzing,
> But of a' the bewattled occasions
>   I can tell a real clish-ma-clash thing;
> There was chitties and rabbit's a-plenty,
>   There was terriers too all a-bawn,
> And feegh! what a claaiken an' caleeverin'
>   When we a' started aff in the morn!"

> "Our cat witted climbers got cankert,
>   The rabbits all campled and dadged,
> The gait that we travelled was dowly
>   An' afore verra long all were fagged.
> The rabbits was gloppened, and hirpled
>   When they found thessels back o' behint.

They haggled and all grew very hackled,
   As snott' ring a lot as ye'll find."

"The sun was at first all a-scomther,
   An' a sad tewing darrak it was,
The taystragelts nigh got to swelting,
   It wasna the trod that *I'd* choose
But we terriers laiked and were ranty,
   They thought us a rackle crew,
Nobbut us could clamber so brawly,
   An' laden with paffeldin too!"

"Wait till I read this to owd Wordsworth yonder!" gurgled Brat. "By gum, but its caps a', and clean off t'stick-end like!" And he settled down to produce some more verses.

So the two poets each sat in a tent, composing, while the tatie-pot simmered and the snow fell outside softly, thickly, as if it would fall forever.

Meanwhile Scratch was leading his party up to Camp Two. Conditions became increasingly bad as they climbed. The snow gathered in immense drifts, the rocks became glazed with ice. A savage, freezing wind tore at them; the temperature fell to sub-Artic. They were now in a bitter, battling world of which valley folk knew nothing. The mountains, far from being the friendly giants they looked from below, had turned into killers.

The cats and the terriers climbed grimly, leaving their marker-flags as they went. To gain Camp Two they had to climb the second of the great peaks along the ridge to the H.K.P.; Camp Two would lie in the hollow between the second and third peaks of this main ridge.

The racing, screaming wind drove the falling snow forward in great curtains, drawn one after the other across the mountain faces, shutting them from sight. The wind fought the animals and the animals fought the wind. They could no longer see their way and climbed by compass bearings, but the rocks of this ridge were magnetic and the compass-needle swung wildly without sense of purpose. The animals sank into snowdrifts from which they had to struggle hard to free themselves; each step forward was a battle.

Scratch saw, to his alarm, that his companions, Oliver and Tibs, were nearing exhaustion, even the stout little terriers were clearly reaching the point where they could not go much further. The light was fading quickly and very early; soon it would be dark. Cats and terriers were roped together: Scratch had Hamish second on the rope. He now waited for Hamish to reach him and said, "I don't like the look of things, Hamish. I can't see any help for it, we'll have to bivouac for the night and hope for better things in the morning."

"Aye," said Hamish. "It's the only thing to do. I wonder if we can get up a tent in this wind?"

They found a place amongst the boulders that seemed more sheltered than the rest of the cruelly wind-swept mountainside; Oliver, completely worn out, collapsed amongst the rocks and lay helpless, Tibs was in a not much better state. Jack Russell was also worn out; he had very short legs and had to leap high with every step he took in the snow, which was very wearing indeed for him.

Scratch, Bits and Rabsie tried to set up the bivouac tent. The tent, caught by the wind, flapped, slapped, struggled and leapt like a giant flounder on a fisherman's line. The animals fought it back, and at last for a moment thought they had it secured, but the wind came charging again in a furious rush, there was a tremendous crack, and the bivouac tent went flying off, a mad giant bird.

"There's nothing left but to shelter as best we can among the rocks, lads," said Scratch as cheerfully as he could, but with a sinking heart. He had a terrible feeling that real disaster might be very near at hand. To show his fears, however, would have been the worst thing he could have done; he tried to be bustling, though his paws now were so cold they had no feeling in them and everything he tried to lift up seemed to weigh a ton. Oliver and Tibs lay sunk in torpor. Scratch gave Jack Russell the job of lighting the high-altitude gas cooker and making hot soup from chicken consommé cubes. Meantime he tried to get through a radio S.O.S. message to Felix in Camp One, while Rabsie and Bits wedged boulders together with snow in an effort to provide some kind of protection against the blizzard.

Scratch had no success with the radio. No response was coming from Camp One. He gave up trying and helped Rabsie and Bits to build the wind-break.

They piled their rucksacks and gear inside the makeshift barrier to give themselves extra protection; they put on all their spare clothing and bundled up Oliver and Tibs. They then drank the hot soup; Tibs was able to feed himself, but Oliver had at first to have the soup spooned into him by Scratch while Bits and Rabsie chafed the young cat's paws. Presently Oliver showed signs of reviving a little. Scratch then ordered Hamish to play his bagpipes and Hamish, a brave little figure in the night and the storm, began playing *The Gay Gordons*.

But there was really very little to be happy about. Oliver grew cold and dangerously drowsy again, Tibs complained of pains, Jack Russell was shivering so hard he couldn't keep still. He was sitting on a biscuit-tin and his shivers made the tin rattle; for a while they couldn't understand what this odd sound was. "You've got pebbles in your pipes, Hamish," said Bits. "Och, nonsense!" said Rabsie, "how could he have?" "Well, what is it then?" They searched to see what the noise could be and at last traced it to the tin of biscuits. This gave them something to laugh at for a moment or two, but then the laughter died and once again they were left to gloomy thoughts of the night, the cold and the blizzard. Scratch wondered how many of his party would last out until morning.

Scratch got Rabsie, Bits and Jack Russell to curl up with Tibs and Oliver in their survival blankets, then he and Hamish rolled up in their survival blanket on top of the rest. In this way Scratch trusted they might all come through the night.

The other animals, worn out, fell asleep quickly, but Scratch lay very much awake. He tried to think what old H.C. would do if he found himself in the same desperate situation.

A hurricane-lamp, wedged between two boulders, gave enough light for Scratch to see how quickly the snow was piling up onto the barriers, the boulders, himself and his comrades under their blankets. The lamp illuminated a small patch of darkness and this was full of whirling, dancing snowflakes; a tiny piece of the whole snow-spinning, wind-raging rest of the night.

And as he lay staring into this patch of light Scratch suddenly saw a face. It was the face that Felix Mouser had described the evening that he had been so scared. It was a bright golden-red, with lots of gleaming, sharp white teeth and a long pink tongue curling between the teeth. The face had dazzling narrow green eyes that caught the lamplight and quivered like fire. Scratch felt his own eyes narrow and burn as he watched this fiendish mask; he felt his fur rise along his spine and his tail stiffen and twitch, his ears flatten back and his whiskers vibrate.

In short, Scratch felt a fight rising up in him.

A snarl collected somewhere deep in his belly and tore into his throat. His lips wrinkled back, baring his teeth, his tongue rolled up, his claws came out. A terrible voice yowled a challenge, he knew it was his own voice; the same instant he found himself spitting and coughing with fury, sailing through the air straight at the red and toothy Face.

Scratch had no idea what the Face was; whether it had a body or not, whether it was real or just a nightmare. All he knew was that he must fly at it and fight it, so fly at it and fight it he did.

The Face proved to have a body attached; a lithe, slender, furry body with a big, soft tail like a brush, plumy white tagged. It also had long, thin black-stockinged legs and nervous, skipping paws. Scratch had expected to land clean on top of the Face and he had his hind legs doubled up under him ready to kick out, scratching as he landed, but the Face and its slim body flicked sideways as Scratch soared through the air and so the cat landed in the snow, which burst round him in white fragments, like spray. The Face gave a mocking yappy laugh and did a sort of light little waltz across the rocks. "Ahaha! Not so easy!" laughed the Face. "Catch as catch can!"

Scratch, furious, charged the Face. The Face laughed more than ever, the neat little feet performed a fandango in the snow and Scratch found himself skidding two or three yards on his nose. He gathered himself up, spitting out snow now as well as fury; the yapping laugh sounded behind him, he spun round, glimpsed the Face, hurled himself again at it, the Face floated off, feather-light and rapid, but so close that for an instant strange whiskers flicked across Scratch's eyes. Scratch pulled himself together; he knew that if he got too angry he fought wildly and to fight wildly was useless. He *would* get this Face! He coiled himself into a taut knot of muscle; the Face, legs, tip-toe feet and waving brush, did a sort of mocking ballet-dance on top of a boulder, finishing up with a dizzy display of *entre-chats*.

"Righty-oh, Rudolf Nureyev, I'll settle you!" hissed Scratch, and sprang at the dancing figure, unleashing himself full-length with the speed and force of a thunderbolt. Normally animals turned tail and fled in horror when Scratch sprang at them like that, but the Face merely laughed lightly and vanished; the boulder rose up instead, so it seemed to Scratch, and dealt him an enormous blow. He saw a trail of giant stars, bright pink, yellow and blue, like rockets on Guy Fawkes' night; they came swooping close and then died, delicately and softly, leaving behind them a furry blackness into which he dropped, head-first, as a conjurer's egg is dropped into a black velvet bag.

Then, perhaps the next minute, perhaps years later, he did not know which, Scratch felt something icy cold pressed against his snout and paws; a voice was saying, "Hey, wake up! Hey, come alive there! Hey, young spitfire!" Scratch opened his eyes. The Face, very close, looped the loop and then fixed itself, right way up, very near to him. It wore an eager, friendly expression. A neat paw patted a little ball of snow in his face. "There, *that'll* revive you!"

Scratch struggled to sit up. He heard Hamish's voice, "There, easy now, easy." He turned his head, which seemed about to split, and saw Hamish. Scratch raised a shaking paw and pointed at the Face. "It, it's a Th-thing," he stammered.

"It's a fox," whispered Hamish, "a braw mountain fox."

"Red Rowan Lightfoot," said the fox, leaping up and making a dashing bow. "At your service. And if I may say so, it looks as if you and your friends here are in need of some help."

"You're dead right, mate, we are," said Scratch.

"Aye, we are that," said Hamish.

"Then let's see what can be done," said Red Rowan. "Can you stand up, young Spitfire, or did you quite knock yourself to bits against that rock?"

Scratch stood up carefully and shook himself.

"I'm orright," he said.

"Champion," said the fox. "Though I must say, if you make a habit of that kind of behaviour you soon won't have many of your nine lives left."

"Why didn't you say who you were at the start?" said Scratch. "It woulda saved me a lotta trouble."

"How was I to know you'd go off like a fire-cracker, just because I looked at you?" said Red Rowan. "After all, a cat may look at a king, so why can't a fox look at a cat without the cat going mad? Anyway, there's my paw; shake it. For I like the way you fly at a chap, I really do; it shows spirit. I daresay it's anti-social, but I'm an anti-social kind of a fellow myself, as no doubt folks will tell you if you mention my name. Well, who cares about 'em, anyway? I do you the compliment of taking you as the same sort as myself, so shake paws, young Spitfire."

They shook paws. Scratch said, "My name's Scratch. Scratch Sharp."

"Grand," said the fox. "Couldn't be better. And now let's get you and your friends under decent cover, for this is a rare bad night to be lying out in the open."

So saying, Red Rowan sprang up on a rock, raised his head and gave three sharp, ringing barks. "That'll fetch the rest of the lads to give a hand," he said. He leapt lightly down from the rock. "Hey diddle diddle, the cat and the bagpipes," he said. "When I heard them playing, Aha, I said to myself, yon's that Hamish McCall, the Scottie from Newlands; what's he doing on my mountain playing the bagpipes to himself on a wild night like this? So I came to look. Good thing I did, too."

"You've said it," replied Scratch. "I'm thankful you did."

As he spoke he noticed one, two, three, four, five then six, seven, lean figures come slinking out of the night. They, too, had red faces, sharp white teeth, fiery eyes. They wore jaunty tattered hats, rabbit-skin jerkins and huge knives strapped firmly to their stomachs; as Scratch looked at them he wondered if he really felt so thankful, after all, that Red Rowan Lightfoot had heard Wee Hamish McCall playing the bagpipes in the wild night.

CHAPTER EIGHT

RED ROWAN'S BORRAN

THE FOXES LED the cats and terriers to a small encampment in a sheltered dug-out under a vast boulder. It was cramped for space and the smell of foxes was dreadful, but otherwise it was most snug. There was no sign of Manx Scoop's rabbits: Red Rowan fed his guests on chicken stew.

After they had eaten, the exhausted animals curled up and fell asleep. Scratch was still not absolutely easy in his mind, but there was nothing to be gained from wearing himself out lying awake half the night fretting, so he rolled himself into a comfortable ball and was soon asleep like his companions.

And indeed next morning it looked as if the Expedition had quite fallen on its feet. Red Rowan was the friendliest of creatures; his one wish seemed to be to help the climbers. After a good breakfast Red Rowan led Scratch and his party to the site of Camp Two; the foxes assisted the cats and terriers to get the camp organized and Red Rowan offered to guide them next day to a suitable place for Camp Three.

Scratch now tried once again to contact Felix on the radio; but he could not get any reply to his signalling. "Must be out, though heaven knows what he can be doing," growled Scratch. He then tried Base Camp and got Tom. Scratch told him about the foxes; Tom sounded dubious. "Don't trust 'em too far, Scratch. They have a bad name, foxes, you know." "Oh, they're orright," said Scratch cheerfully, "and their Leader's a real good geezer." "Well, just remember that foxes have a bad name." "Right, I'll bear it in mind," said Scratch, rather impatiently. There the conversation ended.

He seemed a thoroughly engaging fellow, this Red Rowan Lightfoot. Scratch had already begun to think the talk about foxes, how they could never really be trusted, never really made friends, never came right out in the open, and so on, was nothing but idle prejudice. "It's like all these things," said Scratch to Hamish, "when you get to know a person properly you find out they're quite different from what you've been told. I like this Red Rowan; worth his weight in gold."

Hamish smiled politely and said, "Och aye."

"Well, what have *you* got against him?"

"He's verra guid company, a verra guid talker, an expert mountaineer," said Hamish, "but . . ." His voice trailed off.

"Seems perfectly on the level with us, far as I can see," said Scratch.

"Och aye."

"I like him."

"Aye."

To get more out of Hamish on the subject of Red Rowan seemed impossible. Clearly, Hamish didn't trust the fox, but precisely why not Scratch couldn't discover. "Hearsay and gossip have blacked poor old Red's name," said Scratch to Oliver, "but I think he's a great geezer, meself."

Red Rowan and his seven foxy friends helped cats and terriers get all the gear sorted out at Camp Two; in the evening the cats put on a sort of supper party with tinned salmon, tinned turkey, chocolates, and toasts drunk to the H.K.P. in catnip. The foxes were genial; told amusing stories, sang racy songs. They were a desperate looking lot, with names full of flavour: Dirky, Rigg, Snipe, Scree, and two jolly half-grown cubs, Benn and Binks. Binks was very greedy and rather fat.

"They're young chaps to have with you in a wild place like this," said Tibs.

"Aye," said Dirky, "we train our young ones early. A fox's life is a hard one, mister. Nothing ever gets handed us foxes on a plate. The weakest still goes to the wall in our way of life."

"Those young fellows don't find the mountain that bad," grinned Red Rowan. "It's what you're used to that's half the battle. They were born on this mountain and they'll live their lives on this mountain; it's home to them. Cold times, hard times, lean times, they'll learn to take as they come. As long as they're free and owe no man a living, that's all they care. A fox is his own master."

"Hear, hear, hear!" yapped all the other foxes.

"A wild lot," said Rabsie. "Aye, a wild lot."

The foxes, relishing all the food that was placed before them, eyed the rest of the Expedition stores and gear eagerly but passed no comments on what they saw. They were very polite.

The cats, who had read a great deal in the newspapers about cat-eating foxes, soon felt completely at ease with their new acquaintances. Obviously these foxes weren't cat-eaters! The terriers grinned and cracked jokes with the foxes and the foxes grinned and cracked back; if there was little love lost between terriers and foxes they were forgetting it for the time being.

The following morning Red Rowan and his henchmen were astir very early; they cooked breakfast for everyone, using the Expedition bacon and eggs freely. Binks ate eight rashers and six eggs. Scratch decided to overlook it. Red Rowan, after all, was going to guide the Expedition to the site of Camp Three. And after that, said Red Rowan, Camp Four!

Between Camp Two and Camp Three lay another peak. Cats and Terriers, led by Red, reached its summit by a long cornice-lipped ridge, on either side of which plunged terrible precipices. Scratch was more than thankful to have Red Rowan with him, for although these mountains were untrodden country for the cats, Red Rowan knew his way perfectly and led the animals across snowfields, up ice-filled gullies and over wastes of boulders and scree without an instant's hesitation. Scratch carefully marked the route with the little flags.

At last the party stood on the top of the peak. The sky was heavy with cloud which swirled above and beneath them in a sea of white vapour, giving everything an unreal, dreamy feeling. Tibs handed round portions of Kendal Mint Cake and Oliver photographed the party.

The air smelt of more snow, very soon to fall. "We'd best push on, lads," said the fox. "There's a storm brewing."

The terriers reshouldered their loads, cats and dogs roped up once more, Red alone refused to fasten himself to the rope, saying, "I can manage without that." He bounded down the long steep slope leading off from the summit; he seemed to skim over the slippery snow-coated rocks, but the other animals found the way difficult indeed.

The wind began to race, tearing across the mountain with a nasty wailing, dealing the animals buffets and blows. "Are we nearly there?" asked Scratch. "I don't like the look of this weather much."

"Well, we've some distance to go yet, and that's a fact," replied Red. "Some way to your Camp Three site that is. But if you find the notion agreeable, I know of a grand big borran near here that me and my lads often use; we could spend the night there very well, or as long as we need to stay for the storm to blow itself out, come to that."

"Grand big what?" asked Scratch.

"What we foxes call a borran. A cave under the rocks."

"Sounds fantastic," said Scratch. "Let's go."

"Just one thing," said Red. "I don't want the way to the borran marked with yon little flags. We foxes like our hide-outs kept private."

"Fair enough," agreed Scratch. "No more flags."

Without more ado Red Rowan led the party off among the rocks, along a dizzy little track with screes pouring away from it, then up a gully that seemed almost sheer, then under a vast slab of granite that hung over the heads of the animals like a black wall of doom, then he vanished.

"Blimey, something's swallered him," said Scratch, looking round.

"I don't fancy this place," said Tibs. "Creepy."

"Aye," said Hamish. "Gives me the heeby-jeebies. Shall I bark at it a wee bit?"

"Barking's going to do a fat lot of good," said Scratch. "Keep your bloomin' barks to yourself, mate."

"No harm meant," said Hamish, wagging his tail.

Then suddenly they heard Red Rowan laughing, the sound coming from somewhere near their feet. They looked down and saw a crack in the rock; through this crack peered Red's laughing face. "Foxed you that time!" he said. "Thought I'd turned into thin air, didn't you? Well, come on down; there's a bit of a difficult step, like, as you first get in, but after that it's easy."

One by one the animals squeezed through the crack; the terriers leaving their loads outside. Inside it was dark and for a moment or so the animals couldn't see a thing; then their eyes adjusted to the darkness and they saw a steep little drop, quite sheer, below them. Down this they slithered. Then came a long passage, getting narrower and narrower and the roof lower and lower all the way. At last the passage dwindled to a small hole through which they had to squeeze on their stomachs. Then, to their amazement, they were in a great rock-walled cavern, lit by a huge fire which blazed in the centre of the floor, the smoke twining up to escape through a hole high above. The place was furnished with odd pieces of antique oak furniture, a dresser with rows of pewter plates and mugs, several big four-poster beds with mattresses and pillows and bolsters and blankets and handmade quilts jumbled and tangled in glorious unmade muddles. There were racks of beautifully oiled and polished muskets and sporting-rifles and blunderbusses and pairs of duelling pistols, and shining cutlasses and swords and daggers. There were old shields and enormous helmets. There was a Roman standard with an eagle shining on it, a huge curved drinking horn set in silver, a wolf's skull grinning, gold necklaces, looped for decoration, hanging from old iron hooks; and there were ancient green glass bottles, and pony-shoes, and gold crosses set with pearls and rubies, and glittering urns and ewers, and a show-case full of eagles' eggs. And there were kegs and barrels and big stone jars. And on the floor and in dark corners were unpleasant quantities of gnawed bones.

There were also foxes galore, including the seven Scratch and his party had already met.

"Well, well, come in and make yourselves at home," said Red Rowan. "You're among friends, here, remember. Very good friends."

The foxes piled hospitality upon the cats and terriers; meat pies and patties, tatie-pots, sides of bacon, legs of lamb, devilled kidneys, roast duck and chickens, grilled voles, toasted beetles, smoked salmon-trout, herb omelettes and potted frogs'-legs. They poured cider from the stone jars and bleaberry-wine from the barrels and foxglove-brandy from the kegs. There was no end to it. They played fiddles and guitars and a piano-accordion and one of them performed upon a set of musical stones. They yapped and howled and wailed and yowled and danced reels and jigs and fandangos. Hamish paced up and down in his swinging kilt, piping his famous pibroch, *Wee Hamish is Awa'*. As the evening wore on he became less steady, he tripped and lurched and bumped into things, at one point he tried to put the wrong end of a bagpipe into his mouth. Then he took two cutlasses from the rack on the wall and began racing round the hall barking and giving horrible Highland whoops and yells. Bits and Jack Russell tried to stop him. "Take your paws off me, useless Sassanachs!" yelled Hamish, waving both cutlasses at once. Bits and Jack Russell fled. Scratch and Red Rowan tried in their turn to calm Wee Hamish. "You don't want those nasty sharp things, Hamish, you might cut yourself," said Scratch. "Dinna be sae daft," said Hamish. "Come on, old chap, let me have them," crooned Red Rowan. "Leave me be, foxy,

I'm going to do a wee dance," said Hamish.

He put the cutlasses on the floor, cross-wise, and then began a Highland fling, placing his little round paws very neatly between the cutlass blades, whistling the tune between his teeth and barking every now and again. He hopped and skipped up and down, up and down; apparently he intended keeping it up all night.

The foxes were enchanted; suddenly they all had the same idea at once. They leapt at the walls and tore down every cutlass and sword in the place. Thus armed, two apiece, they ran into the middle of the hall, laid their weapons, crossed, on the floor, and began dancing crazily.

But this general excitement merely drove Hamish on to wilder things. With a blood-curdling shriek he picked up his two cutlasses and waving them above his head he began to spin round and round like a top, clashing the cutlasses together as he spun.

The foxes at once followed suit. The other terriers and Scratch, too, were whirling round and round, waving pairs of swords, but Oliver had got out his ciné-camera and was trying to film the mad scene, while Tibs, with whom bleaberry-wine disagreed, retired to a dark corner, climbed up on a four-poster bed well out of the way of the dancers, and sat there glaring gloomily at the wildly revolving, whooping, cutlass-waving Hamish and muttering, "How like an idiotic dog!"

Hamish spun ever faster. Then he jumped on to a barrel, twiddled round on it, jumped down again, ran to another barrel, jumped on it, twiddled round, and again repeated this performance. All the other animals followed his movements. Then Hamish ran at a shield on the wall, leapt up and gave it a mighty thwack with a cutlass; all the others ran to thwack it. Then Hamish, with a tremendous whoop, picked up one of the giant helmets and dropped it over his own head. There was a loud clang! The helmet thudded to the floor, completely covering Hamish, as if he had dropped a neat metal prison-house over himself, which indeed he had. The other animals crowded round, laughing. The helmet swayed; there was clearly a terrific fight going on inside it as Hamish battled to get out. Muffled barking could be heard and rude exclamations.

"Shall we leave him awhile?" suggested Red.

"Whew! I think we better," said Scratch.

After this things calmed down a little; Dirky sang a mournful song with a lot of howling in it and everyone else howled too. The cats wailed. The noise was sad and very loud and so they all sat with their muzzles pointing up to the ceiling, their mouths wide open, enjoying a great long-drawn sorrow. Hours afterwards, just as he was about to fall asleep, while Red Rowan howled and sobbed a heart-rendering solo above the snoring bodies of the rest of the company, Scratch thought of taking a peep at Wee Hamish under his helmet. Scratch managed to raise it; there lay Hamish curled up asleep like an infant pup. Scratch tried to put the helmet back over Hamish again, but it was so heavy he dropped it instead on his own toe; whereat his voice rose in a series of ear-splitting catterwauls that quite deafened Red Rowan, who stopped howling and shook his head two or three times, in a bewildered sort of way.

CHAPTER NINE

YOU CAN'T TRUST A FOX

SCRATCH WOKE NEXT morning feeling dizzy and bad tempered; he stood up slowly with his fur on end, raised his tail upright, arched his back, quivered his whiskers, extended his claws, snarled, and looked round for somebody to pick a quarrel with, but everyone else was asleep. The fire was out, the cave was cold and dark, lit only by a finger of grey light coming down the hole in the ceiling through which the smoke had risen the night before.

Scratch shuddered. "What a gloomy place! Blimey, what a night! Old H.C. would have a fit if he knew."

Suddenly there was a frenzied barking and Hamish came dashing into the great hall. "Help! Help! Help! A Yeti! A yak! A polar bear! A monster!"

He scudded out again, barking fit to explode. Scratch raced after him.

Hamish galloped up the long passage, barking in a piercing voice which echoed backwards, quite deafening Scratch. When he reached the steep step to the entrance-hole Hamish leapt up wildly, missed his footing, fell, picked himself up and dashed back along the passage again. He and Scratch met full tilt and knocked one another flat. Hamish jumped up barking more than ever. Scratch rose spitting mad.

"You silly twitch-faced terrier!" yowled Scratch. "You gone barmy? Can't you pipe down? Cor, my head!"

"Help! Help! Yak! Snowman! Monster!" barked Hamish. "Come quick! Hurry! We're being attacked! Help!"

He once again galloped to the entrance-hole and this time managed to scramble out. Scratch followed. There was a furious din of barking going on outside. Scratch pulled himself up the step and looked round. The white world beyond the hole dazzled him for a moment. The air too was full of clots of flying snow, kicked up by Hamish who was dancing madly about, barking with fury and quivering with rage and fear before a most extraordinary creature, big as a bolster, white and tremendously shaggy. It stood braced stiffly with legs spread out, blinking at Hamish from under a snow-tangled fringe of eyebrows and hair.

"Yak! Yeti! Polar bear!" barked Hamish, jumping up and down. "Grrh! I'll eat you! Get out!" And, obviously terrified that the strange animal would attack him, he skipped several steps nearer to Scratch.

"Garn, Hamish!" cried Scratch, scornfully, "it's a sheep, a great dirty old sheep what's bin snowed up all night!"

"Sheep indeed! It smells of—nasty! Nasty! Yeti! Polar bear!" barked Hamish as before. "I'll kill it! I'll give it socks!"

"Go on then, mate, give it socks," said Scratch, cheerfully. Hamish danced round the sheep in a wide circle, then made a short rush at it, then bounded back again. The sheep started barking too.

"Yap, yap, yap!" cried Hamish.

"Woof, woof, woof!" replied the sheep.

"Yowp, yowp!"

"Wuff, wuff!"

"Bow-ow-ow!"

"Woo-woo-woo!"

Scratch, helpless with laughter, rolled in the snow, clutching himself. "Oh lor, oh blimey, darn idiotic dogs, they'll be the death of me! Did y'ever? Oh cripes!"

"Yak! Yak! Yeti!" repeated Hamish. "I'll bite you! Grrh!"

"Woof, woof, bite you meself," replied the sheep, indignantly.

Hamish gave the strange animal another, harder look, ran at it, sniffed it, then scuttled across to Scratch, who was still rolling in the snow, weeping with laughter. Hamish licked him excitedly. "I say, I say, I've found out what it is. It's a dog!"

"Good old Hamish! You don't say!"

"But it is! A snow-dog!"

"Ye're daft," said the snow-dog.

"Hello, hello! How are you? Hello!" yapped Hamish, dancing back to the snow-dog.

"Hello yourself," said the snow-dog, wearily.

"I'm Hamish McCall. McCall's my name. Hamish McCall."

"I know," said the snow-dog, even more wearily.

"How d'you know?" snapped Hamish. He danced back to Scratch. "He says he knows who I am! How can he know? We've never met before, I swear it." He leaned close to Scratch and whispered hoarsely behind his paw, "You stand by, ready to help, while I investigate this fella." Hamish, moving jerkily and stiffly, his tail up and very twitchy, then stomped back to the stranger.

"Hello."

"Hel-lo!" said the stranger, horribly bored.

"You say we've met before?"

"Aye."

"Where? Come on, you just tell me where."

"Och, I can't be bothered. I want some breakfast."

"So you won't tell me, hey?" Hamish hopped back to Scratch. "I was right. There's something verra fishy about this. I dinna like the smell of it at all." He hopped back to the snow-dog. "Now, come on, where is it we've met before?"

"Och, Hamish!" sighed the snow-dog.

"Ye canna tell me, can ye? Because, be-cause, ye've never set eyes on me in your life! So there, my canny rascal. Wuff!" And Hamish waltzed round the snow-dog and then ducked in quickly and nipped him neatly above an ankle. The dog yelped, "Ow!"

"Teach you!" barked Hamish.

"This is taking a joke too far, Hamish McCall!"

"Joke? I'm nae joking. Want another nip?"

"Hamish, stop it!" shouted Scratch. "Can't you see who it is?"

"Aye," said Hamish. "Deacon Brodie hissel', straight from the Tolbooth! Ha ha!"

"Verra witty, verra witty indeed," said the other dog. He gave himself a mighty shaking, the snow flew out of his coat in a small personal blizzard. For a moment he disappeared in it; then there he stood, Rabsie the Aberdeen, glowering at Hamish who fell back a step, perfectly astonished.

"Aye-ee, Rabsie mon!"

"And who is Deacon Brodie the noo, hey?" snarled Rabsie.

"Rabsie, where've ye been to get snowed-up so? Jings, I never recognized ye!"

"While you lot were carousin' and drinkin' and beating it up in yon borran, I was out here, guarding the Expedition equipment," growled Rabsie. "That's what I was doin'. Sat by it a' night, I did. And all I'm greeted with in the morn is a wee daft West Highlander barkin' at me and shoutin' insults. Yak! Yeti! Deacon Brodie!"

"Och, Rabsie mon, ye're a wee jewel, a wee dog in a million," crooned Hamish.

Scratch added his praises, "Hamish is dead right. You're the greatest, Rab, you're the champ."

"Those foxes," said Rabsie, "they're a tricky lot. I don't trust 'em and neither should you, Scratch."

"Ah, they're orright," said Scratch. "Decent lotta blokes. You mustn't judge a geezer by his looks, Rab."

"And what d'you judge him by, then?" snapped Rabsie.

"Why, by how he behaves, and all that," said Scratch. "They're a friendly, helpful lot, these foxes. And Red's a real great guy. One of the best."

Rabsie snorted. "We'll see," he said. "We're a long way from home and dry yet."

"Ah come on Rab, we're doing fine," said Scratch. "We're all but at Camp Three, with Camp Four coming up. And a

socking great cave full of booze and grub at our disposal.
It's a dead fall, mate."

But all Rabsie would say was, "We'll see."

The other animals now came, in ones and twos, out of the
borran. Red Rowan came last. He squatted down in the
snow, gave a stupendous yawn so that he seemed about to
swallow himself, then scratched himself hard behind his left
ear with his left hind foot. Then he sat up very straight,
grinned and opened his eyes wide.

"Grand morning," said Red Rowan.

The other foxes were also stretching, yawning and
scratching themselves like fury. It made the cats itch to
watch them. "Foxes are full of fleas, always," murmured
Rabsie.

"Oh, fleas yourself," growled Scratch. He moved over to
Red Rowan. "Well, Red, boy, what are your plans for
today?"

"Camp Three," said Red, "after that it depends on the
weather. I smell more snow on the way."

"Aye," said Dirky. "More snow on the way." He sniffed
the air, long thoughtful sniffs.

"Aye," said the fox called Rigg, staring into the far distance where tall dark mountains and clouds lay together in
a high heavy bank. "There's rough weather coming,
Skiddaw way. And the wind's northerly. There'll be worse
before there's better."

"Aye, aye, aye!" chanted the other foxes together.

"Then we better get shifting," said Scratch.

"If you'll take my suggestion," said Red Rowan, "you'll
use my lads from now on as porters. The way ahead is very
rough and your terriers will find it dowly going, as we say
in these parts."

"Dowly going yesel'," snapped Jack Russell. "Us terriers
come from these parts too."

"Aye," said Red Rowan courteously, "and you're a grand
lot of lads, no one denies it. But put a fox and a terrier on
country like this and the fox will have the terrier beat every

time. How can it be otherwise? We're natural-born fell racers, everyone of us. No one denies a terrier goes well on these hills, but a fox, by his very build, must go that much better."

"Red Rowan Lightfoot, famed for the gift of his gab," said Jack Russell, sourly.

"Let's not argue," said Tibs. "If Red Rowan's good enough to offer the services of his foxes . . ."

"If we foxes are good enough to offer our help!" snapped Dirky. "Red Rowan's not my boss! If I want to help you, I will, and if I don't I won't, so remember that, you cat witted chitty. As for Red Rowan, he can shift for hisself, one way or t'other; he's nowt to do with me."

"Come on, Dirky, yon Tibs meant no offence," said Red Rowan. "We all pull together in this," he added, in a slightly more meaningful voice.

"Aye," said the other foxes, "all together, Dirky." Their eyes shone and their long pink tongues curled out between their gleaming teeth. Oliver got a bit closer to Scratch. The foxes had such a lot of teeth!

"Then what happens to us terriers? We take it easy, do we?" asked Bits.

"Us weak lot get carried up on stretchers, likely," said Jack Russell.

Red Rowan took Scratch aside; they had a short conversation. The other foxes continued to yawn, scratch and grin; the terriers stood uneasy, trembling a little with anxious feelings about they didn't know quite what. Then Scratch called them to him and said, "Red Rowan has had what I think is a real good idea. There's no doubt, like he says, that from now on the foxes will make better porters, what with one thing and another; you terriers, on the other hand, can still be very useful . . ."

"You surprise me," growled Rabsie.

Scratch thought it best to ignore this.

"As Red Rowan points out, Camp Two is lying unprotected . . ."

"Owt in it to protect!" snarled Bits.

"Expensive tents and so on," said Red Rowan. "A certain amount of gear."

"There's some very larky lads around these parts," grinned Dirky. "Not all the foxes up here are straight 'uns like us. Think what happened to Manx Scoop's rabbits."

"What *did* happen to Manx Scoop's rabbits?" asked Tibs. No one answered.

"Anyway, you terriers can be most help at this point guarding Camp Two," said Scratch. "Us cats and foxes will press on up. In a day or two we'll send down a message telling you what's the next step. Okey-doke?"

"Aye," said Hamish, dourly.

"Aye," said the other terriers, in the same flat tone of voice.

In a short while the foxes had loaded themselves with the Expedition equipment, while the terriers made their personal things into small packs, to return to the lower camps. The two groups of animals were now ready to go their respective ways: cats and foxes up, terriers down.

"Well, lads," said Scratch to the terriers, "I'll be in touch with you in a day or two."

"Aye," said Wee Hamish.

"This is by far the best way to do things," added Scratch. "Have the H.K.P. climbed in no time."

"Oh aye," said the terriers.

"See you then, lads. Mind how you go!" said Scratch, confidently.

"Aye," said the terriers. And, with polite little salutes, they turned towards Camp Two, while the cats and foxes moved off in the opposite direction, Red Rowan Lightfoot leading them.

The way he took them proved to be difficult indeed. Snowfields steep as the roofs of houses, rock walls hung with icicles, narrow snow-bridges spanning deep crevasses, dizzy ledges across the faces of cliffs; on and on, while the weather changed steadily for the worse. Scratch said, "This is a long march you're taking us, Red."

"Aye," replied Red, "I told you yesterday it was a goodish step, like, to Camp Three."

So on they went, while the wind raged and whistled and snow started to fall. Scratch was quite lost, but trusted to Red Rowan, who trotted along like one who came up into these parts every day. The three cats, Scratch, Tibs and Oliver, were roped together and had to make good use of their ice-axes and crampons; the foxes scorned rope and axes, but lilted along like feathers, in spite of the loads they carried. When they came to particularly steep, slippery places they held one another's tails and thus hauled and pulled each other up or lowered one another down. They skidded and slid and laughed and yapped; it all seemed a joke to them.

Although the cats were all first-rate climbers and in splendid condition they found they could barely keep up with the foxes who, as Red Rowan had claimed, were unbeatable on the mountains. They had the hardihood of the terriers coupled with the agility of the cats.

Faster and faster went the foxes as the day wore on and the weather grew worse. They stretched out their brushes, using them like rudders to steady themselves in the wind, now and again whisking them round and round as if to help drive themselves along.

The snow was now whirling so thickly in the air that the cats could not see more than a yard or so ahead. Faster and faster went the foxes; Scratch lost sight of them. He called to them to slow down. But no reply came. He shouted again, "Stop! Wait for us!" The wind swept his voice away, the snow raced round him and his two companions. They staggered on, following the foxes' footprints, but the snow fell so fast and thickly that these became covered before the cats could trace them. The cats grew desperate; they tried to run in a frenzied attempt to catch up with the foxes again, but the snow made running impossible and in any case the cats had no longer any idea of which direction to follow. At last Oliver fell flat on his face, exhausted, thereby jerking Tibs and then Scratch to a halt. Scratch dug his ice-axe hard into the snow and then leaned on it, panting. All too clearly, and far too late, he saw that the foxes had tricked him.

Tibs helped Oliver to his feet; the two cats struggled towards Scratch. When they reached him he turned a white face towards them; white with the snow clinging to his eyebrows and whiskers. "I'm sorry, lads," he said. "This is my fault."

"They haven't gone and left us, have they?" faltered Oliver.

"Yep," said Scratch. "They've scarpered."

"Filthy lot," said Tibs.

"They always say you can't trust a fox," said Oliver.

"Now we know," said Tibs.

"I was a right twit not to believe it in the first place," said Scratch. "Yet who woulda thought that old Red–?" His voice died away.

Tibs put a forepaw round Scratch's shoulders. "You weren't to know," he said. "He took me in, too."

"And me," said Oliver. He sank down in the snow. "I can't go any further," he said. "I'm all in."

"Can't stay here, kid," said Scratch. "If we stop here in this blizzard we've had it."

"They've got the tents, the food, stoves, sleeping-bags–" said Tibs. "And the radio."

"Swiped the ruddy lot, mate," said Scratch.

"But what do we do?" wailed Tibs. "We're cut off from everyone. Whatever do we do?"

"Don't panic," said Scratch, perhaps more to himself than to Tibs. "Not–to–panic," he repeated. "Come on, we'll try to find somewhere a bit more outa the wind," he said.

Clinging together the three cats fought their way a few yards down the mountainside, until they came to a small hollow between some boulders. "Here will have to do," said Scratch. "Now next step is to build an igloo."

"I can't," said Tibs. "My paws are frozen stiff."

"Warm you up, this will," said Scratch, determined to be cheerful. Together the three cats tried to heap up snow into some kind of shelter; fortunately they had their survival blankets with them and when at last they could pile no more snow they rolled themselves up in these, huddling together. But they had no food, their shelter was of the barest kind, the blizzard was growing fiercer every moment. Their plight was grim indeed.

Scratch said to Tibs, "Got 'ny Kendal Mint, mate?"

Tibs had a small piece, Oliver had a larger piece, Scratch had a piece. "We'll keep mine for breakfast," said Scratch, "and eat the rest." This they did.

It was by now nearly dark. Scratch said, "We oughta try to stay awake. Let's tell funny stories."

"Are you mad?" groaned Tibs.

"Mad to fall asleep, mush," said Scratch. "Come on, Oliver first. Funny story, kid. Come on, we're waiting."

"No use," said Tibs, "he *is* asleep."

"Wake him up then. He's gotta keep awake."

"I tell you, he's fast off," said Tibs.

"Shout in his ear," said Scratch.

Tibs put his mouth close to Oliver's ear. "Wake up!" he screeched. Oliver stirred, then muttered, "Want to buy a battleship?"

"What's he say?" asked Scratch.

"D'you want to buy a battleship, I mean battle fly," said Tibs.

"*What?*"

"D'you want to buy a flutterbish," said Tibs, drowsily.

"That don't make sense," said Scratch. "Buy a perishing what-d'you-say?"

No answer. Tibs keeled over against Scratch's shoulder. Scratch shook him violently, but the only response he got was to hear Tibs murmur, "Ask the buttershap."

Tibs and Oliver were both beyond conversation. They lay inert, one against the other. Scratch, peering at them in the near darkness, realized that it was hopeless to try to wake them.

But, if they weren't awakened Scratch knew that they had
had it. He himself was beginning to feel drowsy too. The
situation was growing very desperate. Perhaps it was
already too late for there to be any hope of survival or
rescue, perhaps the writing was already on the wall, without
respite, for all three of them. Yet numbed as his brain was
growing, Scratch still realized that any chance of their
coming alive out of this crisis now rested solely with him.

He couldn't lie there, drifting off into a warm, delicious,
yet inevitably fatal sleep. He must make one final, supreme
effort. He jerked himself out of the doze which was softly
lapping him, felt for his ice-axe, fought his way out of the
survival blanket and the snow shelter. He knew that he was
likely to perish doing what he was about to try to do; but if
he remained huddled under his survival blanket he would
perish too. The foxes alone knew where Scratch and his two
companions were and the foxes would not come to the
rescue. None of the Expedition animals knew where the
three cats were, for no marker-flags had been put out over
the final stages of the route taken. The sole hope lay with
Scratch and the possibility that he might make his way
down to Camp Two and the terriers he would find there!

But he had only to face the blizzard and take a few paces
from the shelter he had left to realize how desperately
forlorn that hope was! The night, the dark, the bitter cold,
the driving snow, the tearing wind, the mountain, were all
against him. For a moment he thought of reeling back to the
shelter in despair, but then a final flicker of his fighting self
rose in him; he faced about into the wind and began flog-
ging himself forward. He had a vague, very vague, sense of
the direction he should take, or thought that he should take.
So he slithered and faltered, doing his best to steady and
balance himself with his axe. Then, suddenly, there was no
snow beneath his feet; nothing but space. He felt himself
plunging, hind-feet foremost. He flung up his forepaws,
clutching the ice-axe. There was a shuddering jolt. The axe

had wedged in something. Scratch kicked and scrabbled wildly with his hind-feet, got some kind of purchase. He peered up; a gash of grey light above him showed that he had fallen into a crevasse.

Icy cold came up from the nothingness below him. He moved a little, a piece of ice broke off; for a long time he heard it tinkling and falling beneath him, till the sound dwindled to silence. His heart grew icy as the falling fragment, the great cold wrapped itself round him, his head began to float, or so it seemed to him, from off his shoulders. His claws, clinging to the ice-axe, were numb, the muscles straining in his forepaws and shoulders were already throbbing with strain. He grit his teeth, yet he knew it was pointless to prolong his agony clinging there to the ice-axe. He must drop, as the piece of ice had dropped.

CHAPTER TEN

TO THE RESCUE!

MEANTIME THE TERRIERS struggled back to Camp Two. At first they had great difficulty in finding the way, for there were no marker-flags to guide them; but with a mixture of luck and excellent judgement they at last found the spot where Scratch had agreed to Red Rowan's suggestion to stop planting the flags; here was a tiny orange pennant fluttering in the snow and from thereon the terriers made rapid progress to Camp Two, scampering from flag to flag.

The little blue and orange high-altitude tents lay very lonely looking. The terriers crawled into one, brewed themselves tea, and held a council of war.

"One thing's plain as a lamp-post to me," said Rabsie, "our first duty is to get reinforcements up to Scratch, Tibs and Oliver; for to my mind the foxes aren't to be trusted. Mark my words, Red Rowan Lightfoot is up to some mischief."

"Aye," said the other three terriers.

"He was so keen to have us out of the way," said Bits.

"He was that," said Jack Russell.

"There's a rare lot of them," said Bits, thoughtfully.

"Foxes? Aye," said Rabsie.

"We'll have to get together a guid strong rescue-party," said Wee Hamish. "And I'll tell you what we'll do. Bits and I will go down to Manx Scoop and fetch up him, his mongoose, Sankey and Moody; that will add four bonny fighters to our ranks for a start. We'll send a message to Base Camp, calling out Dr. Black, Alec, Titch and Tiny, to go up to Camp Two without delay. Meantime, you, Jack Russell, hurry down to Camp One and fetch up Brat Wilson and

Felix Mouser. Rabsie stay here just in case Scratch does send down a message like he said. Shift as fast as ye can, lads, for there's a tingling inside o' me that tells me there's nae time to lose."

The terriers acted on Hamish's instructions without a minute of delay. By nightfall Hamish and Bits were in Manx Scoop's tent, drinking hot tea laced with catnip, eating thick ham sandwiches, and telling him, between gulps and bites, about the crisis that had arisen on the mountain.

"We must do something to save those chaps up there and do it fast," said Manx.

Without more talk he began getting into his climbing things; he also strapped a pair of ugly-looking revolvers in a holster round his bulky, muscular body. Sankey and Moody he armed with rifles; the mongoose wore H.C.'s old army revolver belted firmly to his back, it was almost as large as he was so that he looked more like a revolver wearing a mongoose than a mongoose wearing a revolver.

Hamish and Bits had the dirks that they always carried. The party was therefore well armed.

The three rabbits who remained in Manx Scoop's camp were called in and given a message to take at all speed to Base Camp directly daylight broke.

Manx, the mongoose and the four terriers then set out for Camp Two. The rabbits, scared stiff at being left alone in the camp, hid in a dug-out until sunrise; then they crept out and ran like mad to Base Camp.

At Camp One the snow had drifted high round the tents. Brat Wilson, feeding himself comfortably on tatie-pot, had reached the forty-second verse of his ballad on the climbing of the H.K.P., while Felix, sustained by a diet of sardines, lemonade-powder and Kendal Mint Cake, had reached the fourth draft of a thirty-six line ode to the mountain. The poets had each completely forgotten the existence of the other; they had lost all idea of time, even of where they were. Outside the blizzard made a barely noticed background to the poetry with which they wrestled and sweated.

It was with a great jerk then, a real sense of shock, that Felix Mouser found himself suddenly faced by a small, snow-plastered, panting dog who squeezed in under the tent-flap and stood trying to talk and get his breath back both at once.

"Mr. Mouser, sir. There's . . . there's . . . it's a . . . whew!"

"The slim new moon . . . Can't you see I'm busy? Don't want to be disturbed! Slim new moon, Slim. Yes, *slim.*"

"Foxes, sir. A whole army of 'em. Bandits."

"For heaven's sake, have I got to put a notice up outside my tent saying, 'Don't disturb'! Silver-tipped salute the slim-topped, no, no."

"But it's young Scratch, sir, he's in danger."

"Serve him right. Those acrobatics of his aren't mountaineering; he should be in a circus. Now get out, *please.* Tipped, topped, tapped, typed . . ."

"By gum, yon chap is all set for the bin," muttered Jack Russell, crawling back under the tent-flap. "Where's owd Brat? I s'll get some sense outa him."

He crawled into the next tent and at once started coughing, for it was dense tobacco-smoke that he found himself breathing. Brat's voice came,

"An' when they a' stood on t'summit

Twas so clarty they couldn'a see owt . . ."

"Brat, Brat, the foxes 've got yon three cats an' all the gear, like—"

"Ah, gang off wi' ye!" growled Brat. "There's no peace for poets in today's world."

"But, Brat, young Scratch is—"

"By gum, I know what young Scratch is without folks shovin' their way in here to tell me!" barked Brat. "Young Beatnik! That's what yon Scratch—"

So Brat barked at Jack Russell and Jack Russell barked at Brat. They were only small dogs, but each had a great voice.

The tent-flap parted again; Felix tumbled in, all claws and eyes. "Really, have you two dogs gone berserk?"

"Owd Wordsworth in person," said Brat.

Felix, like Jack Russell, began coughing. "My sainted whiskers, what *are* you smoking? Corrugated cow-pat? Last year's hay-rick?"

"Nay, chitty-puss," said Brat. "It's one of O. Slim-Bones' socks, shredded medium."

Jack Russell began coughing even harder. Felix hurried from the tent. He did a small, frenzied dance in the snow.

"Blast those terriers! I *mean* it! Blast 'em!"

Jack Russell came tumbling from the tent, too, choking and wiping tears from his eyes. "Ye're useless, the two of ye, plain daft and useless! I give up!" And Jack Russell sat down in the snow and started to howl.

This fetched Brat out. He barked, Felix catterwauled, Jack Russell howled.

Nonetheless, within the hour all three had left for Camp Two.

If there had been confusion at Camp One when Jack Russell turned up, it was nothing like the confusion that Base Camp saw when Manx Scoop's three rabbits came racing in. H.C. was in the throes of a breakfast argument with Tom Black. The young doctor was desperately worried because he had lost all radio connection with Scratch, neither was Camp One answering. Tom felt he must get up the mountain to find out what was happening. He wanted H.C., now that he could limp on three legs, to go down to Seathwaite to recuperate there. But H.C. was equally determined to go up the mountain with Tom.

"But, sir, you're not really fit enough—"

"Fiddlesticks! I'm going up, m'dear boy, up. When in doubt always go up."

At this point the three rabbits came flying, landing on the cloth amongst the breakfast things. One burned his nose on the tea-pot, another skidded on the butter, a third put his hind leg in the marmalade. It was all very messy, muddled and nasty.

"What the blazes!" cried H.C., staring at the buttery

animal who had landed on his plate.

"Oh, your honour! Oh, your honour!" squealed the rabbit.

"My sainted Aunt Tabitha!" sighed Tom. "Where have all these rabbits suddenly sprung from?"

"Have you got a serviette, your honour?" asked the rabbit who had put his foot in the marmalade.

"A serviette?" asked the dazed Tom.

"Aye, your honour, to wipe yon sticky tack frae me tooty," said the rabbit.

"What nasty, common creatures rabbits are!" grumbled H.C. "One wonders why they were ever invented. Like bluebottles; a creative blunder, Tom, a creative blunder."

"Yes, sir," said Tom, wiping down the marmalady rabbit.

The buttery rabbit climbed carefully off the tablecloth to the ground and rubbed himself up and down on the grass. The tea-pot rabbit sat clutching his nose and snivelling.

"Well, well," said H.C. "and what were you three chaps runnin' away from? More foxes, eh, what?"

"It's foxes, sir, your honour, but not after us. It's your climbers the foxes have catched."

"Which climbers?"

"Why, yon climbing-cat chaps, aloft, seesta. Aye, they'll be cat-cutlets by now."

"Ate, your honour; all ate, same as our poor chaps."

"Tell us what you're trying to say, slowly," urged Tom. The rabbits then repeated Manx Scoop's message.

Tom jumped up. "Good grief, H.C. There's not a moment to lose."

"Not a moment," agreed H.C., jumping up too.

"I'll start up the mountain with Alec, Titch and Tiny," Tom was saying. "Pooks and Yorky Boy can keep an eye on this camp; Yorky can see you down to Seathwaite first, then return here."

Without replying, H.C. limped away to his tent. Tom gave the terriers their instructions, got into his climbing gear, made a last rapid round of the camp, then with Alec,

Titch and Tiny he prepared to start for the higher camps.

Yorky Boy, who had trotted off to help old H.C. get ready for the descent to Seathwaite, now returned from H.C.'s tent looking puzzled. "Sir Hywel's not there."

Tom glanced down the track into the ravine; three little white tails could be seen flashing as the three rabbits careered madly valley-wards, their one thought to regain the safety of the lowlands.

"The old boy's gone with them," said Tom. "You better hurry after him, Yorky. He can't possibly keep up with those bolting bunnies and I don't want him doing the trek to Seathwaite by himself, he's not up to it."

Yorky Boy accordingly bounded off down the ravine. Tom, Alec, Titch and Tiny said good-bye to Pooks and began their climbing.

It was early afternoon when they arrived at Camp One. They found a note left by Felix. "Have gone up to Camp Two. Please follow immediately." Tom and his party pushed on without delay. Luckily it had stopped snowing and the going was a lot easier.

Down at Seathwaite the arrival of three breathless rabbits caused a great sensation. Whiskey Bylines, all agog for a story at last, fetched out a bottle of *Skin Tonic* (or so the label said) and poured the rabbits bumper glasses. They were soon gabbling a fearsome tale of foxes, cat-cutlets, rabbit-pies, blizzards, horror and disaster. Whiskey could not get it on to paper fast enough. "Cat bid for H.K.P. fails. Climbers captured by cannibal foxes. Scores of porters eaten." He opened a bottle of *Pine Bath-Essence*, took a long, long swig, then sat down to his typewriter and began pounding the keys frenziedly.

Presently Yorky Boy trotted wearily into the farm-yard. "Got Sir Hywel Catterwaul here?"

"No. Should we?"

"I was told he'd come down."

"No."

Yorky sighed. "By gum, then he must've gone up."

"You don't mean to say you've lost H.C.?" asked Whiskey, even more excited. "Where? Where?"

"If I knew where I wouldn't be looking for him. Would I?" snarled Yorky.

"Have a drink; you're all in," mewed Whiskey, holding out the *Pine Bath-Essence*. But Yorky shook his head. "You can't bribe me to talk to newspapers!" And he took a drink of water from the runnel in the yard. Then he went back up the ravine towards Base Camp.

"Whoever invented cats," growled Yorky, "was a nutcase."

CHAPTER ELEVEN

RED ROWAN'S PAW OF FRIENDSHIP

SCRATCH, CLINGING TO the ice-axe with benumbed claws, knew that within a matter of moments he must fall into the crevasse. It seemed a stupid way for everything to end, but that was how it was to be.

The numb sensation grew. One of his paws clutching the ice-axe slipped. He tried, sickeningly, to get a fresh grasp on the axe, realized he couldn't. It was quite useless. This was it.

Then two black-stockinged feet appeared, miraculously, and a sharp, very clear voice said, "Hold hard, I've got you!" A rope-sling was passed round his body and, as he finally lost his grip on the axe and fell, Scratch felt himself pulled up short by the rope now belaying him. His sensations were too blurred for him to be aware of the details of all that followed, but soon he was lying on his back in the snow, with a jet sky above him and a very large, three-quarters-full moon set, like a shiny lop-sided dinner-plate, in the centre of it. A neat black paw appeared holding a small metal drinking-cup; Scratch felt his head being raised and a warm, tingling dose of foxglove-brandy was poured down his throat. Feeling very wobbly Scratch sat up and shook himself. Red Rowan Lightfoot was crouched beside him, gulping down foxglove-brandy in his turn. When he had drained the cup he turned big eyes, shining green in the moonlight, on to Scratch, grinned to show all his white teeth, poured out more brandy from a flask, handed it to Scratch and said, "*Skol.*"

"*Skol,*" said Scratch and drank the brandy.

"That was a near thing," said the fox.

"Yup," said Scratch.

Red poured himself another drink, swallowing it in big, slow, thoughtful gulps. "Where are Tibs and young Oliver?" he asked at last. "Down there in yon crevasse, or asleep in some snow-drift?"

Scratch started up, everything very blurred. "Asleep in a snow-drift."

"Any idea where they are?"

"Yeah, I left 'em somewhere up there," replied Scratch, staring vaguely up the mountain. It had stopped snowing, the night was very bright and clear, range after range of peaks glittered round them, an ocean of great, frozen waves. The moon lit everything with cold precision. The mountain on which they stood swept up barely and white like a ridge of gleaming bone. Scratch stared at it, repeating, "Up there."

"Right," said Red Rowan. "Soon as you're thawed a little, up we'll go." It was true that Scratch was stiff with cold; he was glad to have more foxglove-brandy while Red massaged his limbs for him.

"You've saved my life, Red," said Scratch.

"Forget it," said the fox. "If you think you can move we best try to find those other two cats of yours."

Scratch stood up, rather groggily, and did a series of kicks and jumps in the snow to warm himself further, while Red collected the rope with which he had rescued Scratch, looping it as he drew it to him. Then he pulled from the snow the ice-axe to which he had belayed the rope. "We better tie-up together," said Red. "The state you're in, you're liable to go skidding off to kingdom-come." Roped together they ascended the ridge, Red leading and cutting steps with his axe for Scratch in the steepest, most difficult parts.

Tibs and Oliver were lying in deep, dangerously deep, sleep under their survival blankets and the piled snow. Red and Scratch hauled them out and started shaking and slapping them awake.

At last the two cats were stirred enough to grumble and stumble; Red and Scratch dosed them with foxglove-brandy, rubbed their frozen muscles. When they could walk, Red said, "Now we must get you to a tent."

The cats, all roped together and led by Red Rowan, found themselves lurching and sliding down a long ice-slope towards a small orange tent which they recognized as one of their own. Then they were inside it, eating a hot meal that Red rapidly produced, washed down with steaming tea. Scratch found himself wondering vaguely why Red had saved him and his companions so gallantly and what lay in store for them now that they had been saved!

The cats, however, were so dazed after their recent adventure and soon so sleepy with the brandy, food and warmth, that they curled into slumber without asking Red Rowan any questions.

The fox crept from the tent into the keen, brilliant night, climbed a nearby crag to give him extra height and then yapped a volley of ringing cries. From far below on the mountain another fox answered. For a moment or two they exchanged their messages, then Red stole back into the tent, rolled himself up in his brush and went to sleep.

When the cats woke it was late, the sun was high in the sky, the morning was blue and gold and fine, the mountains lay free of all cloud and bad weather, the thick snow spread over them was dazzling to the eye. The cats crawled one by one from the tent and peered blinkingly about them; Red Rowan was frying sausages which sizzled deliciously. He grinned at the cats. "Good-morning; feeling better?"

"Great, thanks. Fine. Fantastic," said the cats.

"Breakfast will be ready any minute now. Meantime, have some coffee," said Red. Scratch commented to himself that Red certainly knew how to make himself at home with other people's stores.

They sipped coffee, stared at the morning-bright mountains, wondered to themselves questions that Red might not be willing to answer even if they were asked. At last, however, Scratch said, "We must all three thank you for being our saviour, Red."

"Not at all," said Red. "If you remember, I said forget it."

"Not an easy thing to forget," said Tibs.

"We'd like to know why—er—you bothered," said Oliver. "After all, it did look awfully, at one point, as if you foxes had scarpered off with our gear and left us cats to freeze."

"Oh aye?" said Red Rowan.

"It jolly well did," said Tibs. "If you hadn't returned to the rescue, Red, we'd have had it."

"Don't mention it," said Red, a little sarcastically perhaps. "All done in the spirit of friendship." He poked with a fork at the sausages browning in the pan. "Nigh on ready," he said.

He busied himself with the breakfast. Oliver muttered to Scratch, "Where d'you think the rest of 'em are?" "Dunno." "D'you think they're really all that friendly?" "Dunno." Oliver stirred his sugar with a tea-spoon, he looked very worried. Scratch gave his shoulder a small, furtive pat, to hearten him. Red, poking hard at the sausages, seemed to ignore all this. Scratch finished his coffee. "Well," he said, "I shall never forget I owe my life to you, Red, and neither will these other two lads here. Damn good life-save it was, an' all." He changed to a lighter tone. "May we ask what's next on the menu?"

The fox replied, "Sausages, hot rolls, marmalade."

"And after that?"

"After that, Camp Four. And after that the summit of the H.K.P., I very much hope."

"Perfect. Couldn't be better."

Red served the sausages. Although they were tinned ones they had turned out very well. Scratch glanced at his wrist-watch. Ten minutes past ten. That time last night, he reflected, he had been clinging to the ice-axe in the crevasse, with no hope of ever eating sausages again. The thought cheered him a lot. They had got out of last night's peril, so why not survive today, whatever today might bring?

He heard Oliver give a slight gasp. Scratch looked at the young cat; he was staring at a long black procession of

distant specks, little moving figures rapidly trotting one
after the other over the top of the skyline, to slide, skilfully
and rapidly, down the snowfield slope above the tent.

Were they terriers coming to the rescue? Or foxes with
heaven-knew-what cunning schemes? The cats peered at the
glissading figures; then the wind carried a musky, acrid
smell across the snow towards the tent and the cats' noses
said, "Foxes" several minutes before the cats' eyes con-
firmed that the approaching animals were indeed the
enemy.

They came sliding, dancing, whisking round the tent;
scores of foxes, all carrying loads of stolen Expedition
equipment. But though their movements were lithe and
graceful enough, their eyes and jaws were grim and when
they saw the cats their ears flattened.

The cats tried to appear as casual as possible; to show
alarm was asking for trouble from the start.

Red Rowan stood up, cocking his ears in a swaggering
style. "Well, lads," he said cheerily, "here you are then."

The foxes drew up in a circle round the tent. They did
not answer Red Rowan's smiles with smiles. "Yes," said
Dirky at last, after a long pause, "we're here."

"Then as soon as we've finished our breakfasts," said
Red, "we'll get started, lads."

"Aye, when we've finished *our* breakfasts," said Dirky,
staring nastily at the cats.

"Haven't you eaten?" asked Red.

"Oh aye, but we're always ready for more," said Dirky.
Several foxes chorused, "Aye."

"Well, lads, there's no sausages left, but there's plenty of
corned-beef and sardines," said Red. Scree interrupted,
"Tinned stuff! We want summat fresh!"

"Aye," said all the other foxes.

"Don't know where you're going to find that, up here in
the snow," said Red.

"Don't you then?" jeered Dirky.

"Cat-cutlets!" said the fox they called Rigg. "Verra

deelishus, cat-cutlets."

"Aye," said all the foxes.

"Depends on the cats," said Red. "If they're youngish, like; haven't had time to grow stringy—"

Oliver felt himself starting to shake.

"But these cats here, you must be daft to think of trying to cutlet them," went on Red. "They're three of the toughest climbers in Catdom; all bone and gristle."

"Make good strong soup!" shouted a fox at the back. All the other foxes roared with laughter. Even Red allowed himself a quick flicker of a smile. Scratch said, "Rum way of carrying on, Red. Rescue us one day; turn round and bump us off the next. It don't add up."

"Leave this to me," hissed Red between his teeth. The fox then turned to the ring of lean red animals, "Lads, there's several ways of looking at this."

"Aye," said Dirky, nastily. "Here's these three cats, which according to your planning should be froze stiff by now, sitting here eating breakfast with you, healthy as they come. Well, one way of looking at this is that you've double-crossed us, Red Rowan; which ain't a healthy lookout for you."

"I had my reasons for saving 'em," said Red, lightly as he could.

"Better if we'd ate yon cats in first place, like we wanted!" barked another fox. The rest chorused, "Aye!"

Oliver shuddered and pressed closer to Scratch.

"What made you save 'em, Red Rowan?" asked Dirky. "We all agreed that the fewer cats in these parts the better. We don't want cats on our mountains!"

"Don't want cats on our mountains!" yelped the other foxes.

"Lads," said Red, and Scratch saw that he had changed from red to dark brown with sweating, "in the first place, apart from all else, as I've said before, anybody who tries eating these cats here will be laid up with the belly-ache. Now, why choose belly-ache when the alternative is to make a name for yourselves and end up rich, eh?"

"Make a name? End up rich? That's likely!" snarled the foxes.

"If this Expedition gets up the mountain you lads will all reap the glory of having had a part in it," said Red. "There'll be handsome rewards all round. You'll be the rich, famous foxes who've trod higher than any fox has trod before. Even you lot have never climbed the H.K.P., have you now?"

"Don't want to neither. It's got evil sperrits," said Dirky.

"Any animal that sets foot on top there will turn to stone," said Rigg. "You know that, Red Rowan."

"There's a lotta queer stones up there," said Dirky. "You can see 'em on clear days. Some's fox-shaped, others dog-shaped, one's like a tiger; or so they say what's seen a tiger. They're all animals that's climbed up there in the past and turned to stone."

"Very convincing," said Red, sarcastically. "Especially the tiger. There's tigers up here galore, tigers galore!"

"Used to be, Red Rowan, used to be in Ice-Age. Sabre-toothed."

"Right then, lads," said Red Rowan. "You don't want to go up there because you might turn to stone. Very well; no need for you lot to go to the top. Get the equipment up to Camp Four; then you stay put and me and these three cats here will go to the top. If we get turned to stone, fair enough. It'll be just what you want; you can keep all the Expedition gear and no awkward questions asked."

"Who's going to ask awkward questions, anyway?" jeered Dirky.

"Some very awkward questions indeed will be asked if these three cats here get eaten. There's a Queen of Catdom, you know, and she's got thousands of soldiers, thousands of airplanes. They'll all come marching and flying over here, wanting to know what's happened to their three famous young climbing-cats."

"And who'll tell 'em?" jeered the other foxes.

"They won't need no telling, not in words they won't.

They'll hear all you lot hiccupping and belching with indigestion; and they'll know what's happened. I warn you, these three cats here are real tough."

The foxes roared with laughter. Whatever might be said against them, they were animals with a great sense of humour.

"Whereas," added Red, when the laughter had died down, "if you leave these cats to go up the mountain and get turned to stone, well then, if the Queen of Catdom starts asking awkward questions you say, 'Aye, Your Majesty, they got turned to stone just like all the other animals who've tried going up there, seesta, sabre-toothed tiger and the lot.' "

"And all this swag?" asked Dirky, nodding at the loads of gear.

"If we don't come down from the top you can scarper off with it and hide it. Nobody will find it among these mountains," said Scratch. "And if we do get back alive you may keep it anyway, as a just reward for helping us get up."

"Can't be fairer than that, lads," said Red Rowan.

The foxes talked amongst themselves. Red, pretending hard that he wasn't worried, kicked an empty sausage-tin round the tent and whistled, *D'ye Ken John Peel?* The three cats sat tense and anxious, stretching out their claws, then pulling them in again, and twitching the tips of their tails.

Then Dirky turned slowly towards them and yapped, "Right-oh, we'll get you safe to Camp Four if it's agreed that whatever happens we foxes keep all the gear."

"O.K.," said Scratch, "that's agreed."

"Yes, agreed," said Tibs.

"Agreed," said Oliver.

"Shake on it?" said Dirky.

They all shook on it, solemnly.

There were a large number of foxes and the paw-shaking took some time. In the middle of it most unexpected sounds were heard; three gun-shots rang out loud and clear, followed at once by the bagpipes. The foxes looked up at the

ridge above, and over the skyline came Hamish piping and
Manx Scoop waving his revolvers, Sankey and Moody
brandishing their rifles, Bits his dirk, and the mongoose
leaping all four feet up in the air at once and down again,
swearing in Urdu, his revolver on his back. They lined up
for a moment on the skyline, then Manx Scoop shrieked,
"Charge!" and down they all came in a great rush. The
mongoose lost his footing, landed on his back, and slid at
top speed all the way down on his revolver, as if it were a
bob-sleigh. As he neared the bottom of the slope he began
spinning round and round as he slid.

The animals charging down the slope found that they
couldn't stop as they neared the bottom. Oliver flung out
his arms and caught Bits, Tibs clutched at Hamish and
received a nasty accidental jab in the eye from a bagpipe,
Scratch caught Sankey, Sankey grabbed Moody, and Red
Rowan received Manx Scoop at full tilt. The cat and fox,
clutched together, flew head-over-heels backwards into the
snow. As they staggered to their feet the mongoose, horribly dizzy but game as ever, rose from the ground, twiddled
drunkenly in a couple of lop-sided circles, trying to recover
his balance, saw the lurching, tightly partnered Red Rowan
and Manx Scoop, squealed, "I come, sahib, I come!" flew at
Red Rowan, missed him and sank his teeth, for a second
time in his life, into the rear of his luckless master.

Manx yowled, spat and danced in agony, the mongoose,
eyes tightly closed, hung on uttering his famous fighting
whistle between his clenched fangs; Scratch grabbed hold of
the mongoose, shrieking at him to let go, while Oliver, Tibs,
the terriers and all the foxes howled with laughter until they
were reeling helplessly with the tears running down their
cheeks.

This chaos of sound and movement lasted several
minutes. Then, as Manx leapt and capered in pain and fury,
he caught his toe in a guy-rope of the tent and fell heavily.
There was a deafening explosion, the mongoose sailed up
in the air, still strapped to the revolver, then plummeted

down again and vanished into a snow-drift. Manx and Scratch both stood feeling themselves to see if they were hurt. "What happened?" gasped Scratch at last.

"Revolver went off," said Manx. "A miracle we weren't shot."

"Where's Ranjit Singh?" said Scratch, looking round.

"Don't know, don't care. Hope he's blown himself to blazes," snarled Manx.

Oliver and Dirky were digging Ranjit Singh out of the snowdrift. He emerged chittering, "Sahib, sahib, I must return at once to India. Your so-called civilisation is no use to me; I have decided against it absolutely now that I have heard one of your super-sonic bangs."

"Don't be such an utter idiot, Ranjit Singh! That was your own dratted revolver you heard go off!"

"Sahib, I am nonplussed. I did not fire it."

"You were too busy chewing another darn great hole in me, you abject, chump-headed chipmunk."

"Sahib, I am now doubly nonplussed. I see I was absolutely inflicting injury on the wrong person. It was my very gravest error, a sore mistake."

"A sore mistake indeed, you plusfoured wretch," growled Manx. "You're lucky I don't sack you on the spot."

Ranjit Singh bowed low, raising his forepaws to his forehead, pressing them together as he raised them. Manx Scoop sighed and patted the mongoose on the head. "Means well, but is mugwump," said the newspaper-cat resignedly. "Well, where's the war? I thought I was charging into action?"

"No war here, Manx," said Scratch quickly. "All the very best of friends."

Manx looked round the assembled animals. "Well, well," he said. "These mistakes are sometimes made."

"All united in the cause of climbing the H.K.P." said Tibs.

"Aye," said Red Rowan, "cats, foxes and doggy bow-wows all act as one."

"Cut out the doggy bow-wow stuff," said Moody, in a

low voice.

"All act as one forthwith," said Manx, putting away his revolvers. "Who's the Leader of this united Expedition, and what are the Leader's plans?"

"Red Rowan and I are leading this thing together," said Scratch. "As for our plans, we get the gear and climbers up to Camp Four; from Camp Four we send a party to the top of the H.K.P. As simple as that. And now, lads, let's quit the argy-bargy and get on with it."

There was, however, one major worry remaining for Scratch. The foxes had wrecked the radio. Knowing nothing about such things, indeed obviously supposing a radio to be much the same as a dead goose or turkey, they had gnawed and torn it to fragments, so that it was now nothing but a mass of twisted wires and chewed parts. Scratch stared at it in horror. "What on earth . . .?"

"We-e-el," explained Dirky, "we worried it a bit, like. Took out its chitlins."

So Scratch and his party were still cut off from the rest of the Expedition.

Laughing, joking and full of good cheer the foxes set off with the other animals for Camp Four. As they were about to start Red Rowan sidled up to Scratch. "May I have a word with you?"

"Sure."

Fox and cat dropped back a short distance behind the others. Red said, "You won't go back on your agreement to let 'em keep the gear, will you?"

"I don't go back on agreements, Red."

"If they don't get what they're promised, I'll be for the high jump as well as you cats."

"Repeat, I don't go back on agreements."

"They're not a bad lot really, but they're foxes, and let's face it, the fox has no friends but his fellow foxes. Everyone's agin the fox, so he's agin everyone likewise. But me, I've said I'm your friend and I mean it."

"Even though I'm not a fox?" grinned Scratch.

"You've got guts," said Red. "Give me a chap with guts and I'll take off my hat to him. If I give him my paw of friendship I'll abide by it. I might have a moment or two of weakness; we all have 'em, but put to the real test once I've given my paw to a chap I'll stick by him."

"Thanks, Red," said Scratch. "And you've proved it, too."

"Shake again, to cement it?" said Red grinning.

"O.K. Red," said Scratch. "Cement it is."

The two animals shook paws warmly.

CHAPTER TWELVE

MY MOUNTAIN

THE WEATHER HAD turned fine and clear; Camp Four was set up at the foot of the last great rise of rock-ridge leading to the fifth and final peak, the H.K.P. The sun shone from a cloudless blue sky, the snow glittered. Scratch and Oliver were in first-class condition; poor Tibs, however, had frost-bitten paws. This, alas, meant that he could not be one of the final assault party, which would now consist of Oliver, Red Rowan and Wee Hamish, led by Scratch.

This party would make the assault in two stages: an ascent of the bottom of the summit arête, where they would bivouac for the night, starting early next morning in a bid for the top.

Manx, Bits, Sankey, Moody and Ranjit Singh set up camp on their own some little distance from Camp Four. If the foxes made off with the main Expedition gear (as everyone half expected) while the climbers were on the mountain, Manx would have enough food and equipment in his camp to get everyone, Scratch's assault party included, safely down to Base.

Manx and his companions, on the day Scratch's party set off, spent much time watching the ridge above them. There were four tiny roped figures; Scratch, Hamish, Oliver and Red. They moved slowly; a high wind was tearing at them upon the exposed ridge, making the going difficult. Presently, they disappeared from view: they were setting up their bivouac amongst the rocks.

As the first pale green light touched the tops next morning Scratch put his head out of the bivouac tent and felt the air with his whiskers. A fine day! He woke the others. They drank coffee, nibbled some biscuits, discussed final details.

The earliest light was strengthening, the east was filling with gold as the four climbers began their ascent of the final shoulder of the H.K.P.

In Manx Scoop's camp everyone was astir, watching the shoulder through binoculars, and when at last the four little figures were seen climbing the knife-edge of the arête a loud cheer went up.

"They've got a fine day for it anyway," said Bits.

"Yes, it should go today, it should go today," said Manx. "They have a fine and true party and a good and lovely day and the mountain should go."

Since no animal had reached the summit before, the climbers had no idea of what to expect on this last section of the ascent. To Scratch's surprise they met with few diffi-culties until, at the top, they found themselves on a plateau strewn with hundreds of huge boulders, as though a giant hand had strewn them there, a monster fistful. "Ice-age mammoth elephants came up here in a herd and got stoned," said Scratch, laughing.

But it was not really a laughing matter for each boulder had to be climbed over, or a way wormed between it and its neighbour, and this was long and difficult work. However, at last the climbers had struggled over these obstacles and found themselves within a few steps of their goal, the summit of the H.K.P.! They raced across the final stony yards of ground, wild cheers of victory rising in their throats; but then, as one, they all stopped, silent and still, gazing at a most marvellous peak that had suddenly sprung into view ahead of them. A majestic dome of rock turrets, spires, pinnacles and pisgahs, supported by enormous but-tresses and gashed with gullies as deep as doom. The animals had never seen anything like it.

"Well," said Scratch at last, "here we are standing on the highest known peak in Catdom but, blimey, if you ask me, it's that mountain there wot's the real cat's whiskers!"

"Jings, it's the dog's dinner!" yapped Wee Hamish.

"It's the real fox-trot, is yon," said Red Rowan. "This one we're on is a few feet higher, maybe, but I'm telling you, yon's the mountain where the spirits dance on midsummer night, and the fires are lit and the magic done."

"And that's where we'll hoist our flag," said Scratch. "Where the magic's done. Come on, you lot."

Between them and the magic summit stretched a chasm, spanned by a sharp-edged bridge of rock. Along this they went, to be stopped by a face of smooth, out-sloping slabs, ending in an immense black overhang. To the right was a miraculous landscape of precipices, soaring and plunging, divided by three vertical gullies. Across this immense rock architecture ran two narrow ledges.

Scratch led the party down to the first ledge which they crossed cautiously. It led them into the third of the gullies; up this they climbed. Large stones poised, ready to fall at the merest touch, starting an avalanche. This gully led into a cave, suspended, it seemed, in mid-air. Scratch discovered a way out of this by climbing the back wall. He gained the top of the wall, reached his paws over the edge, groped for a good hold, got it, pulled himself up. He rose to his feet and discovered that he was on the summit of the mountain.

One by one the others followed him.

They stood silent and motionless for a dazed moment; then returned to life, embraced each other, purred, barked, mewed. The cats pounced and capered in delight. Red Rowan and Hamish bounded, rolled in the snow patches and scratched up fountains of frozen spray which swirled upon the wind in sparkling puffs and streamers.

Below them spread the world, wide and clear. The mountains rolled in battalions to the flat green coastline; beyond lay the glittering blue sea with more mountains, a great way off, clouding the horizon. Over the vast panorama of plains, sea, and cloud-like mountains floated the real clouds, remote and tranquil.

"Now for the ceremonial," said Scratch. He and Oliver

planted in the snow a small silk flag of Catdom. "We name this peak Mount Felicia," cried Scratch, "after our glorious Queen Felicia of Catdom, whose mountain this is and all the lands and seas to be viewed from it. Long live Queen Felicia!"

Red Rowan next performed a ceremony. He swept a circle in the snow with his brush, scattered rowan berries in the circle, buried a small hack-pudding (made of sheep's heart, suet and dried fruit), placed a piece of white quartz to mark the spot where the pudding lay, cocked up a hind leg and carefully sprayed the stone. "Scaur Fell," he said. "The fell of bare rock. Magic mountain of foxes."

Hamish, very slowly and deliberately, walked up to the stone, raised his leg and paid a penny on the stone. "*My* Mountain."

Scratch and Oliver exchanged glances. "Canines," said Oliver wearily.

"Don't know better," said Scratch.

Red was glaring at Hamish. "That was a doggone stupid thing to do. Now you've ruined my magic circle. If you get turned to stone, serve you right."

"Jings, that stone talk is nobbut a lotta nonsense."

"Maybe, maybe not," snapped Red Rowan, "but all these mountains have spirits you know, that's a fact, and no spirit is going to enjoy being piddled on by a common terrier."

"Common terrier yesel'!"

"Hamish, remember where you are," said Scratch sharply. "You're a highly honoured dog to be up here; behave."

Hamish was glancing round uneasily. "Stone dogs, cats, sabre-toothed tigers! Jings, I canna see them."

"A mountain must always be treated with respect, else it will get its own back," said Red Rowan. "Mark my words, you'll suffer for this, Hamish McCall."

"Whisht," sniffed Hamish, "dinna fash yesel', my superstitious poultry-thief." He took a small flask from his hip-pocket, walked back to the stone, sighed, unstoppered the flask. "Here's a wee washit o' whisky for your precious magic the noo," he said and poured a slow trickle of amber spirit over the stone. "Nae Scot can do more than that!" he added, fiercely, scowling horribly at Red Rowan.

"Thank you, lad," said Red Rowan, grinning. "All is forgiven."

Hamish snorted, raised the flask to the sky and barked, "An' here's a health to Ben Nevis!" He put the flask to his mouth, tilted his head back in a long, long swig. Then he restoppered the flask, placed it in his pocket, picked up his pipes, gave a preliminary wheeze or two on them and swung splendidly into *Wee Hamish is Awa*.

He was still playing when the time came to leave the mountain. The animals roped up, Hamish gave a final skirl of pibroch, all eyes turned for a long last look at the little fluttering flag, the circle, the stone, then moved further to the watchful neighbouring peaks, the broad horizon, the silver sea. Then one by one the climbers disappeared over the lip of the wall into the cave. The mountain was alone again.

Scratch and his companions didn't stop at their bivouac place but pushed on, excited by their victory, all the way to Manx Scoop's camp. As they slithered and staggered, all but exhausted, down the final pitches of the shoulder, they saw another party, led by the unmistakable, stump-tailed figure of Manx Scoop, coming up to meet them.

Suddenly no longer so tired, the four conquerors of the mountain leapt to greet their friends, shouting the tremendous news of victory as they ran. What a hugging, thumping of backs, cheering, laughing, and even crying with joy! "Blimey, that's a real summit!" cried Scratch. "Fantastic!" mewed Oliver. "A magic mountain!" yapped Red Rowan. "*My* Mountain!" barked Hamish.

Then back to Manx Scoop's camp they all went. Soon the four climbers were telling the great tale of the ascent of Mount Felicia–Scaur Fell–*My* Mountain, while champagne corks popped and Ranjit Singh prepared a savoury-smelling chicken speciality. After this delicious supper Hamish took his pipes and began composing a new pibroch, *Wee Hamish Atop the World.*

The animals arrived at Camp Four early next morning, or rather where Camp Four had been, for not a trace of it remained. The foxes had vanished, and with them every bit of equipment.

"No harm done," said Manx. "After all, we were more than half expecting this."

"Those lads would never wait for us to come back," said Red, "because they all believed, every fox tod of 'em, that we were going to end up stone-statues. Nobody waits for a stone-statue."

Manx was anxious to get his dispatches safely to his newspaper before Whiskey Bylines discovered that the mountain had been climbed. Bits and Sankey offered to act as runners and carry the dispatches down to Rosthwaite post-office in record-time; there Manx had a very reliable stoat waiting who would telephone the messages directly to the *Cat Times.* So the matter was settled. Sankey and Bits were to go with all speed to Rosthwaite; the other animals to Base Camp.

They reached Camp Two that evening. No one was there. However, Tom Black had left a note, 'URGENT. Believe climbing-cats may be prisoners of foxes. Have gone with strong party to fox cave H.Q. Please come at once, repeat, AT ONCE, to reinforce us. Tom Black.'

"This could put the fat in the fire," said Manx Scoop. "Lead to nasty complications with the foxes."

"Aye," said Red. "The lads won't welcome that kind of invasion of H.Q. We'd best get along there fast as we can, before the blood starts running."

"You're dead right, mate," said Scratch. "Let's start moving. And hope we arrive in time."

CHAPTER THIRTEEN

IN FEAR AND TREMBLING

Tom Black, Alec, Titch, Tiny, Jack Russell, Felix Mouser, Brat Wilson and Rabsie had searched in vain for the climbing-cats and had finally despaired of finding them. At last Rabsie suggested that, if they had been taken prisoner by the foxes, they might well be at the cave, of which he gave graphic and horrible accounts.

"I didna gang in it mesel', ye ken; I guarded the equipment outside, but Hamish told me about it and jings! ye never heard the like! Such goings-on, such barbarities! It was Sweeney Todd, Billy Burke an' Sawney Bean a dozen times over!"

"Good grief!" said Felix.

"Doesn't sound too good for our three chaps," said Tom.

"Wh-what'll we d-do?" asked Felix, his teeth chattering. "G-go b-back and get h-h-h-h—" He gulped; blew on his hands as if to warm them (the sun was shining and it was very hot amongst the rocks), and said, "Ch-chilly."

"Chilly who?" growled Jack Russell. He disliked the faint-hearted.

"C-cold up here," said Felix.

"Rats," snapped Jack Russell.

"You were saying to go back and get? Get what?" asked Alec, with a hint of sarcasm.

"H-h-h—" began Felix.

"H-h?"

"—elp," gulped Felix.

"Help from who? Chilly?"

"Ah, stop it you lot!" said Tom, sorry for the poor baited Felix. "This isn't going to get anything done. Could you find your way to this fox cave, Rabsie?"

"Aye," said Rabsie. "Any place I've been to once, I can find again."

"Then march," said Tom.

Rabsie, true to his word, led the animals unerringly to the foxes' cave. There were no signs of life around the entrance except (if these can be called signs of life) several rabbit bones, picked very clean and gnawed at the ends. Poor Felix, whose knees were trembling so that he could scarcely walk, made a small snowball and pressed it to his forehead. He was of a gentle, pacific nature. One of the reasons he had become a mountaineer was because battling with mountains was so much more civilized than fighting his fellow creatures.

He looked at his companions. A strange, hard tension had gripped them. The terriers, who loved a scrap (except for poor Tiny, on his coupling chain with Titch), were getting out their dirks and examining them. Titch was trembling and straining, his mouth wide open to show horrid fangs and shining scarlet gums. Felix noticed with a shock that something, sometime, had chewed his lips away and his muzzle was scarred in all directions. He was an ugly-looking devil of a dog, in every sense. The only thing that prevented him rushing headlong into the cave was the reluctance of Tiny to move at all; he had sat down and was protesting in muffled, but none-stop accents. Felix glanced from the terriers to Tom; even that highly intelligent cat, who devoted himself to the science of healing, had a new and nasty glitter in his eyes.

"What's the next step, Alec?" asked Tom, in a low voice. "Creep in and take 'em by surprise?"

"It's rare to take a fox by surprise," said wise old Alec. "If there's anyone at home they know we're out here, sure as bones are bones."

"Let me go in, let me!" snarled Titch.

"Last thing we want," said Alec. "Let you loose amongst 'em, Titch, and a fight will be on without more ado. We need to be a bit more subtle than that. Foxes are cunning animals and cunning should be met by cunning."

"Rot it, are we going to *talk*!" gasped Titch. "You all gone soft?"

"If we have to fight we'll fight," said Rabsie, calmly. "But there were a lot of foxes in there t'other night and if there's the same number now they'll be three to one at least."

"Pooh, what's three to one ?" sneered Titch. "I been five to one afore now and left 'em licking their bites. There was that time in Deer Bield Borran–" He left his sentence unfinished, happy at the memory.

"If we can avoid a fight–" began Felix.

"If we can avoid a fight we will," said Tom. "And if we can't, well, then we'll give 'em an account of ourselves they won't forget. The question is, do we go in together, or send in an emissary?"

"Send in a steaming what?" snapped Titch, impatiently.

"I-I'll b-be the emissary," said Felix. "We p-pacifists are not necessarily c-cowards, you know."

Tom patted him kindly on the shoulder. "Good old Felix."

"Where's a white f-flag for me to c-carry? Anything white will d-do. Got a hanky, Tom?" said Felix, praying his legs would carry him into the cave.

"White *flag*?" snapped, snarled, yapped and yelped all the terriers together, furiously indignant. "By gum, we've not started fighting yet!" said Jack Russell. "Let alone reached the stage of white flags!"

"And it's not us who'll need white flags!" growled Alec.

"But how will they know I'm f-f-friendly?" said poor Felix.

"You're unarmed," said Tom, "and you simply walk in and say–er, 'How d'ye do?'–I think," he added. "Look round, you know, and see which of 'em seems the leader. Address your remarks to him."

"Sort of 'Dr. Livingstone, I presume?' " said Felix.

"Well, sort of."

"And then?"

"Well, if they're friendly you come out again, saying you want to fetch your companions. If you don't come out within five minutes we'll come in."

"Oh – er – well – I sup-p-pose that'll d-do," said Felix. "As it were. So to sp-speak, and so f-forth. Well, g-good-bye, then." He stood up slowly. Tom said, "It's the best plan I can think of. I mean, if they're friendly they'll be perfectly willing to meet the rest of us. And if they won't let you fetch the rest of us, well then, it'll rather speak for itself, won't it?"

"I suppose so," said Felix. He took a step or two towards the mouth of the cave. He hoped he did not look so fearful as he felt. "Well, so long," he said. "Hope I don't make a bish of things." He lowered himself into the cave.

With his cat's eyes he had no difficulty in seeing his way along the dark, narrow, low-roofed tunnel that stretched ahead of him. But he was almost suffocated by the dreadful reek of foxes. "*Quel* pong!" muttered Felix, whose happiest years as a schoolmaster had been spent at a famous cats' prep-school where he had picked up a jargon which he always found himself using in moments of crisis.

The passage dwindled to a small hole, like the entrance to a rabbit-burrow; Felix lay down flat and wriggled through. As he emerged he heard a youthful tittering and a cracking sound. He looked up slowly. He could hardly believe his eyes.

He was in a great vaulted cavern lit by a fire in the centre of the floor. The place was a mixture of a stately-home long neglected, with antiques, heirlooms, bric-a-brac and cobwebs galore, and an old battlefield where nobody had ever troubled to tidy up. There didn't seem to be a live fox in the place, though the foxy smell was strong as ever. Also, there was this silly giggling and the cracking noises.

Felix rose to his feet and peered more closely into the shadows. Something moved. His blood turned degrees colder; he stared in horror. Then his eyes made out an enormous oak four-poster bed, with tatty, ancient, crimson velvet hangings. At the foot of this bed sat a very fat fox-cub, cheerily gnawing and crunching a rabbit bone. Behind him, perched on a pile of dirty-looking pillows, sat another cub, giggling like crazy.

"Oh - er - hello," said Felix, taking a few steps towards them. "Anyone else at home?"

"No," said the cub with the bone.

"You - er - live here?" asked Felix.

"Aye." With another crunch at the bone.

"Who else lives here?"

"All of 'em."

"Who - er - is all of them, exactly?"

The giggly cub giggled harder than ever. The fat cub chewed a noisy mouthful of gristle, swallowed it with a gulp and said, "Why, Red Rowan, Dirky, Rigg an' all."

"Any idea where they've gone?"

"Gang ayant wi' Red Rowan."

"Any idea when they'll be back?"

"No."

"Mind if I bring a few of my friends in?" asked Felix, as casually as he could. "We've come to visit."

The two cubs looked at one another, the giggler exploded into a cascade of giggles. The fat one said, very off-hand, much more interested in his bone, "Go ahead."

Felix groped his way back to the cave entrance. "It's most odd," he told the waiting animals. "They all seemed to be out apart from the two cubs. Of course, it may be an ambush."

"Exactly," said Tom. "Everyone on their guard. Felix, lead the way. Play it all very cool until I give the signal, if I have to give a signal."

But it seemed the cubs were indeed speaking the truth. They were the only foxes at home. And all they knew of the whereabouts of the other foxes was that they had gone up the mountain with Red Rowan.

"What happened to the climbing-cats?" asked Rabsie.

"Dunno."

Tom, Felix and the terriers sat down by the fire, still very much on their guard and very thoughtful. At last, Felix said in a low voice to Tom, "This isn't getting us anywhere. Hadn't one of us best go back to Camp Two to see if anyone has turned up there with some kind of news?"

"Good idea," said Tom. "Tell you what. Give it just a while longer here and if nothing turns up then you'd best nip back to Camp Two and see if anybody is in evidence there."

The fat fox-cub now came staggering to them with a large pewter platter on which were piled joints of cold roast rabbit. "Like some?" he grinned.

"That's very kind of you," said Tom.

The other cub brought bleaberry-wine. Felix said, "What's your names?"

"I'm Binks," said the fat cub. "Yon youngermer's Benn."

Binks and Benn proved generous hosts. They offered helping after helping of the roast rabbit, which was very good, and beaker after beaker of wine. Tom said, "We're eating you out of house and home."

"No matter," said Binks. "There's rabbits a-plenty in yon pantry." He grinned broadly, the thought clearly a happy one for him.

"Aye," said Benn. "And don't they squeal when we walk past, eh Binks? They think it's their time come. Will be soon, too, eh, Binks?"

"Aye," said Binks. "We bin fattening 'em; they was very scrawny wi' all that carrying packs up the mountain. But they're nigh on ready now."

"Aye," said Benn.

"Pies, patties, stews!" said Binks, rolling up his eyes and rubbing his tummy. "Spit-roasted wi' wild-thyme and stuffed wi' onions! Potted an' eaten cold! Grilled on skewers atwixt slices o' bacon! Simmered in cider wi' crab-apple rings and dried rose-hips! Minced and served wi' mushrooms on toast! An their l'al kidneys devilled for breakfast!" He laughed, then heaved a long, loving sigh. "I'm so fond of rabbit," he said.

"Sounds like it," grunted Jack Russell.

Felix nudged Tom. "D'you think we're eating our porters?"

Tom pulled a face. "Dunno. They taste very good."

"I'd rather not be eating 'em. I mean, I don't mind eating a rabbit who is a complete stranger, but one of one's own employees—"

"Our lot got back to Seathwaite safely, I'm pretty sure of that. We may be eating Manx Scoop's."

"Sounds to me like they're the lot that are being fattened up," growled Jack Russell.

"Well, who *are* we eating then?" mewed Felix.

"Oh, don't worry so, Felix!" said Tom. "You'll give yourself an ulcer. Does it matter who you're eating? Rabbits are rabbits and there to be made use of."

"All the same," said Felix, "it was understood that the porters shouldn't be eaten. A sort of gentlemen's agreement, and all that."

And he refused any further helpings.

He also, rather to Tom's surprise, encouraged the two fox-cubs to drink some bleaberry-wine. They grew even more giggly, made silly jokes. "What's woolly and walks on four legs?" "I don't know," said Felix. "A sheep?" "No." "A caterpillar?" asked Rabsie, after some reflection. "How could it be? Caterpillars have billions of legs, sorta suckers, seesta," said Benn, scornfully. "What then? We give up." "Why, a woolly jumper!" "But a woolly jumper hasn't any legs!" cried Felix. "Oh aye? My mistake," said Binks. Benn rolled on the floor, laughing. "He lied about the legs," he said. "That's the joke, see? Like another? We've lots more."

But in the middle of the next one, which was about a weasel and a sack of potatoes, and sounded as if it were going to be rather rude, the two young foxes started to yawn, forgot what they were saying, lay down suddenly and limply, rolled their brushes round themselves and went to sleep.

"You've got those two innocents tiddly," said Tom to Felix, reproachfully. "That's a nice way for a schoolmaster to behave."

"Innocents!" said Felix. "A couple of young rogues. Come on, let's find those rabbits. And maybe, who knows, poor Scratch and Co. into the bargain."

Investigation proved that several lesser passages ran out of the great cavern, as well as the main passage. Most of these came to dead ends. Three of them, however, led to exits, very useful to know; each exit opening upon a different part of the mountainside.

The borran seemed endless; the passages twisted in all directions, with cave after cave, none near the size of the enormous central one. Some of these caves were empty, some were used as lumber-rooms, some contained dismal piles of bones. Some were stocked with kegs and bottles of wine, some had hooks in the ceiling from which hung hams and smoked sausages and black puddings. And one cave, but only one, had its door locked.

"Manx Scoop's rabbits, or our climbing-cats?" muttered Tom. Brat Wilson put his nose to the crack under the door. "If you ask me," he said, "it's rabbits."

The door was of very stout wood, with a heavy padlock. Felix rattled the padlock. From within came a chorus of terrified squeals.

"You're right, Brat," said Felix. "It's Manx Scoop's rabbits. But how we get to 'em is another matter."

"Perhaps if we all heave together we can break the door down," suggested Tom.

But in spite of every effort they could not break the door down, or pick the padlock, or find any other way of reaching the rabbits.

"Not a hope," said Tom. "And never a sign or sound of our poor lost cats anywhere in this grotty, gruesome place. Felix, you better buzz back to Camp Two, see if there's any news there."

Felix, trying not to look too thankful, said good-bye for

the second time that afternoon and was soon glissading down a snow-slope as fast as he could go.

To his complete astonishment when he reached Camp Two he found H.C. there. The old cat was cosily installed in a tent, opening a packet of digestive biscuits.

"Why, Felix m'boy, this is a pleasure!" mewed H.C. "Got the others with you?"

Felix rapidly outlined the situation so far as he knew it. H.C listened gravely.

"Better join me in a quick cup of tea and then we'll get up to that cave as fast as we can," he said.

"D'you think that'll achieve very much, H.C.? I mean, it might be more helpful if we stayed here for a while to see if any messages—"

"My instincts," said H.C., lifting the little metal teapot he always carried with him on his travels and starting to pour tea, "my instincts tell me to go up. Up to that cave, Felix."

"Yes, sir."

"When in doubt, my boy, always go up. Dear me, this tea has a very odd taste. Very odd indeed. Must be China tea."

"Rather peculiar, sir, even for China tea."

"Never did like China tea; weak, namby-pamby stuff. And these days heaven knows what they do to it with that chap Mao there."

"Give it a stir, sir. See if that improves it."

H.C. removed the teapot lid and began stirring the tea with a spoon. "Heavens, what have we here?"

He fished about with the spoon and slowly drew from the pot a grey woollen sock, sodden with tea. Felix began to snigger.

"Whatever is this?" exclaimed H.C. "One of my socks! How on earth did it get into the teapot?"

Felix was helpless. He rocked on his camp-stool. "I wonder if its fellow is in the pot, too?" murmured H.C. "After all socks generally travel in pairs."

H.C. placed the first sock on his plate, fished in the pot again and produced the second sock. Felix didn't know what to do with himself.

"It all comes back to me now," said H.C. "I'm very expert in the art of packing a rucksack and the art of packing a rucksack, my dear boy, is to make use of every inch of space. For this reason I remember now that I packed a pair of my socks inside the teapot. The teapot, of course, went inside the rucksack. Unfortunately I had forgotten this."

Felix still could not speak. He clutched his sides and sobbed with laughter. He trembled and shook with it.

"I am not surprised that the tea has a rather odd flavour," concluded H.C., "for you see, my dear fellow, apart from anything else the socks were a dirty pair."

It took Felix some time to regain his composure. When at last he felt sufficiently recovered from the wildest fit of laughter he had known since he was a schoolboy, he made some fresh tea. He also apologised for his rude behaviour. H.C. said, "Not at all. Not at all. I can see myself that the incident was not without its funny side." Which sent Felix off again.

And indeed even after the two cats had finished their tea, shouldered their rucksacks and were climbing back up the mountain to the cave, Felix was shaken, from time to time, with fits of muffled laughter as he recalled H.C. fishing the sock from the teapot. The mountain had its lighter moments.

CHAPTER FOURTEEN

HONOUR AND GLORY

THE FOXES RETURNED to the cave, singing. It was the famous old song about the great grey-goose who was stolen by the fox and carried back to his den and the little foxes, as the chorus went, picked the bones-O! Tom and the terriers, seated by the fire in the cave, heard the high-pitched yappy voices echoing, nearer and nearer, along the passage, "Bones-O, Bones-O!" and it was not a pleasant moment.

Then the foxes were there, each one under a vast load of Expedition gear, each one grinning with satisfaction. They saw their visitors and stopped short.

"Well, well, lads," said Dirky at last. "We got company. What a pleasure!"

"I'm Dr. Black of the H.K.P. Expedition," said Tom, rising to his feet with an assumed air of ease. "Red Rowan, I presume?" He held out a polite paw.

" 'Fraid not. My name's Dirky." The fox looked hard at Tom's extended paw as if considering what to do with it; Tom wondered whether he was going to receive a bite instead of a paw-shake. Then Dirky shook it, a hard, slow, not very friendly shake.

"Poor Red," said Dirky, "we won't see his like again in a hurry. He was a grand chap." He heaved off his load. The other foxes followed suit. Tom eyed all the Expedition gear. Dirky said, "Well, and what can we do for you, eh, doctor?"

"We've called to see if you have any news of our three climbers. Scratch Sharp, Tibs Brightstone, Oliver Simkin."

"Aye, poor lads, poor lads. They were grand young chaps, full of fight and fettle," Dirky sighed. The other foxes chorused, "Good lads."

"What's happened to them?" asked Tom, feeling his heart turn over. Dirky said, "They and Red Rowan. By gum, it's a bad end."

"Well, tell us what's happened," snapped Tom. Dirky said, "They're all lined up on yon mountain top, doctor, graven stone images, seesta, graven stone."

"What on earth are you talking about?" said Tom.

Dirky sat down slowly onto a wooden coppy-stool; his distress seemed sincere enough. "We warned 'em, didn't we, lads? Aye, we warned 'em." The foxes yapped, "Aye, we warned 'em."

"It's a well-known historical fact, in these parts, doctor," said Dirky, very seriously, "that any living creature that climbs yon mountain you call the H.K.P. turns to stone. There's stone animals up there, on clear days you can see them; plain as plain, in every detail."

"So our three cats and your Red Rowan went up the H.K.P. and turned to stone, is that it?" said Tom.

"Aye, doctor, that's it."

"They went up, when?"

"Four days since."

"And you've seen and heard nothing of them more?"

"Doctor, since they went up t'ridge towards top, we've heard and seen nowt."

"And so, since they didn't come back, you foxes decided to walk off with all the Expedition equipment, did you?"

Dirky's eyes gleamed very unpleasantly. "Walk off with it! We did not walk off with it. Yon Scratch gave it to us."

"Forgive me," said Tom, "but that doesn't sound very likely."

"Yon Scratch," said Dirky, "told us that if us foxes got him and his lot up to Camp Four safely we could keep all the gear, whether he and his party came back alive or not. That was the bargain he struck. We got him up to Camp Four. So, the stuff is all ours now."

" 'Fraid not," said Tom. "It just wasn't his to give you."

Dirky clenched his teeth in a hard line and spoke through

them. "A bargain's a bargain."

"Aye," said all the other foxes, "a bargain's a bargain."

"I'm sorry, I don't seem to be able to get you to understand," said Tom, who was always very polite. "This equipment doesn't really belong to us climbers at all. It belongs to the Royal Feline Geographical Society who sent out this Expedition. So you see, Scratch was in no position to make such a bargain."

"Well, us foxes mightn't be educated folk," said Dirky, "but in these parts, doctor, a bargain, once struck, is a bargain. We kept our half of it; fair play now, fair play."

"Aye!" yelled the foxes.

"You tell me what you've done with our climbers," said Tom. "There's been some foul play there, if you ask me."

"I told you," said Dirky. "They're stone images, poor lads, stone images."

"But surely you don't expect us to believe *that*!" exploded the exasperated Tom.

"No, not you daft, cat-witted lot," sneered Dirky. "You and yon dirty little dawgs—" spitting out this last word with the utmost contempt.

The terriers began to bark all together in furious indignation. This insult was more than they could stand. Dirky, with a leer, made a cut-throat gesture at them. At once Titch, with a scream of rage, hurled himself at Dirky, pulling poor Tiny head-over-heels in his wake. The next instant Dirky and Titch were fighting like furies, while other foxes leapt to Dirky's aid. Tiny lay down on his back, exposing his breast and belly to the enemy, his paws up, in the classical animal attitude of surrender. The foxes simply stood on him the better to reach Titch. Tom shouted at the other terriers not to join the fight, but it was useless; they rushed at the foxes and in an instant the cave was writhing with a mass of battling animals.

It could not last long, it was too uneven. The terriers fought desperately, but they were overpowered by sheer weight of numbers. The foxes bound them with strong twine and leather straps and lined them up against the wall. Tom, however, was left at liberty for the moment since several animals had been wounded in the fight and the doctor now had the job of patching and bandaging them. Binks took a couple of sheets off a bed and he and Benn tore these up for dressings.

Tom bandaged the foxes first, then he turned his attention to his own party. Dirky snarled, "You needn't spend too much trouble on them, doctor, the short time they've got left on this earth it don't signify if they miss out on the First Aid."

"I hope you'll bear in mind," said Tom very solemnly and loudly and clearly to Dirky, but for the benefit of all the other foxes too, "that this Expedition has the patronage of Her Gracious Majesty the Queen of Catland–"

More jeers.

"AND SO ARE THESE TERRIERS, LOYAL SUBJECTS OF THE QUEEN!" bawled Tom.

A perfect tempest of jeering, with yells of, "Traitors!" "Toadies!" "Scum!"

"And our Queen," shrilled Tom, his voice rising to its highest, loudest pitch, "takes good care of her subjects!"

A gale of horrid, yelping laughter.

"You murder us lot, like you've doubtless murdered our poor comrades, and I tell you, you'll regret it, every one of you!" continued Tom. "Don't think you're too far away, here, for the law to reach you! You'll find out very differently, mark my words!"

"Tie him up," snarled Dirky. "He's done all the doctoring he's ever going to do."

Rigg and Scree tied up Tom. He said, "For the last time, I warn you, the arm of the law is a very long arm."

"Law and foxes," said Dirky, "are further apart than the sun and the moon."

"You'll discover otherwise," said Tom.

"Well, you won't be here to see," said Dirky, "so I should stop worrying, doctor, and start praying instead."

"What you gonna do to 'em, Dirky?" asked Scree. "Chop 'em?"

"Aye! Chop 'em! Chop 'em into little bits!" yapped several foxes. But others shouted different suggestions: "Roast 'em! Pickle 'em! Stuff 'em up the smoke-hole!"

"Well, doctor," said Dirky, "you see we're giving you quite a wide choice. Which way do you prefer?"

"For the very last time let me warn you, solemnly," said Tom, trying to appear perfectly calm, although he realized that the end was only a matter of moments away. "Doubtless you'll murder us in cold blood as cheerfully as you've already murdered our three poor young climbing comrades, but you will regret it, how bitterly you will regret it!"

"For the last time," said Dirky, "we got no fun out of knocking off your three climbing-cats, because we never knocked 'em off. It was all planned; they was to die accidental, like, in the blizzard, but Red Rowan played a double-game and rescued 'em. I still can't think why. Having saved 'em from the blizzard he said to let 'em all go up the mountain; he knew, well as we did, they'd turn to stone. He made off with 'em saying he was going up the mountain too. It was suicide on his part, and I can't think why he did it."

"For two reasons," said a very clear, mocking fox voice. Into the centre of the cave pranced a dapper, graceful, bright red fox, with a swagger and an air of authority which marked him from the rest. "Firstly, because I don't believe in old wives' tales; turn to stone! What a bogey story for a dark night and a windy hearth! And secondly, though I don't believe in fairy tales I do believe in friendship." He turned and pulled Scratch forward into the circle of firelight, then stood with a forepaw resting lightly on the cat's shoulder. "This cat here is my friend, all these cats here are my friends; I said I'd see 'em safe up the mountain and I did, and down again too. I gave my paw on it, and my paw is as good as any bond. The rest of you foxes can't understand that, can you?"

As he finished speaking, Oliver, Tibs, Manx Scoop,

Ranjit Singh, Hamish, Bits, Sankey and Moody pressed forward behind Scratch. They were all armed and looked, to tell the truth, anything but friendly.

Dirky glared morosely at the new arrivals. "Us other foxes struck a bargain too," he said, "and kept our part of it. We gave our paws; at Camp Three we gave our paws. Yon Scratch said we could keep the gear if we got him and his party to Camp Four. We got 'em there. And now we're told we can't keep the gear."

"Who tells you that?" asked Red Rowan, quickly.

"Yes," echoed Scratch, "who says that?"

"I do," said Tom who, although now trussed up like a chicken, still managed to speak with authority. "How can we give these foxes all the gear! It isn't ours to give. It belongs to the Royal Feline Geographical—"

"Oh blow the Royal Feline Geographical!" exploded Scratch. "That's just the kinda cockeyed nonsense I'd expect from the Royal Feline Geographical!" He turned to Dirky. "What's going on 'ere anyway? These animals have got no right to be parcelled up like this. Get somebody to undo 'em all, pronto."

"Ranjit Singh, undo the sahibs, and the sherpas," said Manx to the mongoose. Ranjit Singh put his little paws inside his waist-belt, produced a murderous-looking hunting-knife, and advanced towards the bound animals. Dirky stepped forward.

"Oho, not so fast," he said. "Before you high-handed chitty cats and this ferret here—"

"Ferret!" spat Ranjit Singh. "Ferret!"

"Pole-cat then," said Dirky.

"Pole-cat!" shrieked Ranjit Singh, dancing with all four feet at once in rage. "I am a mongoose! Mon-goose!"

"Never heard of it," said Dirky, with an ear-to-ear, sarcastic foxy grin. "Stoat or weasel, I suppose?"

Ranjit Singh uttered a piercing tea-kettle whistle, slewed round the revolver from his back to his front, jerked it out of his waist-strap, pressed the butt to his tummy, simultaneously slipping the safety-catch, pressed the trigger, shut his eyes and spinning like a top, whistling as he spun, fired all six bullets in the revolver, one after the other. Every animal in the cave flung himself flat on his face.

By a miracle nobody was hurt. The bullets flew into double-beds and flitches of bacon, one embedded itself in an oak linen-press, one went into a bucket of potatoes, one went through the case of eagle-eggs, sending egg-shell fragments in all directions. When he had finished firing Ranjit Singh fell flat on his back and lay there. The cave was full of echoes and smoke and smelled of cordite.

An unmistakable voice was heard.

"What's goin' on here? Celebrations, eh what? Or has every animal in the place gone berserk?"

The smoke cleared to reveal Hywel Catterwaul with Felix behind him. H.C. gazed round at the cats, terriers and foxes, all flat on their faces, save the bound ones, who huddled slumped against the wall, while Ranjit Singh lay toes up on his back.

"How many of this lot are dead?" asked H.C. "Those not dead stand up."

Everyone except the bound animals and Ranjit Singh stood up, slowly, feeling themselves.

H.C. stared sadly at the mongoose. "This little chap seems to have had it. Sorry about that. Liked Ranjit Singh. Spunky little fellow."

"Flaming little idiot," said Manx Scoop. "If he shot himself it's all he deserves. Chump-headed chipmunk." He bent over the mongoose and felt his pulse.

"Best let Dr. Tom look at him," said H.C. "I suppose you've got Dr. Tom here, what?"

"I'm here, sir, but I'd like to be untied."

"Un-what?" For the first time it registered with H.C. that the doctor and seven of the terriers were bound as prisoners. "What foolery is this?" thundered H.C. "Who tied up my medical officer and these terriers in this execrable fashion? By gad, whoever is responsible for this outrage will pay for it!"

At last Dirky spoke. "Well, your honour, it's this way, like. I did. Or rather, me and my fellow foxes did."

"Oh, you did, did you? And what in blazes for?"

"Well, your honour, a bargain's a bargain, and when us foxes strikes a bargain we don't go back on it, oh no! But there's some that do, so it seems. And that's a game me and my mates here don't think much of."

"And I don't think much of finding my M.O. and terriers trussed up like table-fowls by a pack of mangy, smelly, scrawny foxes! By gad, I don't! So undo 'em at once!"

Dirky nodded at Rigg and Scree; they stepped forward and cut the bonds off Tom and the terriers. Tom at once began First Aid on the mongoose.

"And now," said H.C. in a quieter voice, "tell me about this bargain, Mr. Er – Mr. Um–"

"Dirky, your honour."

"Tell me about this bargain, Mr. Dirky."

Dirky once again gave an account of the bargain he had struck with Scratch, concluding, "We got 'em up to Camp Four, your honour. So we kept all the gear. For with us foxes, a bargain's a bargain."

"I see your point of view, see it very well," said H.C. "Unfortunately this equipment isn't ours to give away to people. It belongs to the Royal Feline Geographical Society."

"Yon Scratch made the bargain."

"Doubtless," said H.C. nastily. "From all that I have heard of Mr. Sharp, it is exactly what I would expect him to do. By all accounts he has–ahem–never had much respect for other people's property."

Scratch's fur rose, his tail twitched, his eyes blazed yellow, his ears flattened back. He looked very ugly indeed. But with an enormous effort he managed to control himself. He said, "These old geezers at the Royal Feline Geographical, which d'you think they'd rather have?"

"What?" snapped H.C.

"I say, which d'you think they'd rather have? Us Expedition cats ate by foxes and all the gear swiped, before we ever even climbed the mountain, or the mountain climbed and the gear gone to the foxes in the cause of climbing the mountain? What's these old geographical geezers more interested in?" asked Scratch, scornfully, "keepin' their perishin' equipment, or us climbin' the mountain?"

"Have you climbed the mountain?" asked H.C.

" 'Course we've climbed the flamin' mountain!" yowled Scratch. "What else we come here for? Pic-nics?"

"My dear, dear boy," said H.C., tears springing to his eyes. He went shakily up to Scratch and, before Scratch realized, embraced him. "My very, very dear boy. This is magnificent! Magnificent! Words fail me."

"Make up yer mind," said Scratch. "Kiss me, or court-martial me. Either way won't send me on a heaven trip."

"My dear feller," said H.C., "naturally you're annoyed with me. You have every right to be. Here you are, successfully led your party up the mountain, and all I do is tear strips off you! I'm a silly old fogey, a silly old fogey! But forgive me, I didn't know the facts."

"That's orright, mate," said Scratch, overcome in his turn. "You didn't mean no harm. Just stickin' up for the Royal Feline Geographics. But straight, which d'you think they'd rather have, us dead and ate as cutlets and all the gear knocked off by these here foxes and the mountain unclimbed, or the mountain climbed and us alive and this gear - er—give as a - er - sorta payment, like, if you dig, to these 'ere foxes?"

"My dear Scratch, the Royal Feline Geographics—Geographical Society, will back you on this one to the hilt, to the hilt, once they have been given the full facts."

"I should hope so!" growled Hamish. "Jings, yon Scratch is a braw wee cat if ever I saw one! I dinna think much o' cats in the normal way o' speakin', if ye'll excuse the remark, but yon Scratch is a credit to cats; if a' cats were like him I'd no mind bein' a cat mesel'."

"Hear, hear!" shouted all the other terriers and the foxes.

"Three cheers for Scratch!" yapped Red Rowan.

And the three cheers were given with a roar that made the cave ring again and again.

Ranjit Singh, conscious once more, but still rather dizzy, was taken into a corner and given a severe dressing-down by Manx Scoop. The mongoose then made the company a short speech of apology. He said, "Sahib Scoop is a great cat. He is without doubt the greatest of living cats. Sahib Catterwaul and his party, they are also without doubt the greatest of living cats. To offend such cats is indeed a calamity and with my firing of the sahib's revolver I fear I have caused such offence. I am most heartily contrite for all alarm and despondency occasioned by my most irresponsible outburst and on no account will repeat such regrettable behaviour." He then salaam'd very low until his turban touched the floor, while everyone cheered him, shouting, "Good old Ranjit Singh!" After which Ranjit Singh climbed into a suit of armour, curled himself into a ball inside the helmet and went to sleep.

The foxes, at last convinced that they were to keep the Expedition gear, now began fetching out piles of food, kegs of ale, bottles of wine and brandy. Presently Jack Russell overheard a nasty fragment of foxy conversation: "No need to worry, there's a pantry full; they can quickly be got ready for eating." Jack gave Manx Scoop a dig in the ribs. "Mr. Scoop, your rabbits are about to be ate."

"Well, let 'em loose, let 'em loose!" exclaimed Manx.

"It's not as easy as that," said Tom. "They're locked in a larder; we've already tried to get them out, but the door is padlocked and we can't unfasten the padlock."

"Then we'll break the door down!" snarled Manx Scoop.

"Can't, Manx. We tried it. Tried everything," said Tom.

"We must do something!" exclaimed Manx. "I swore I'd do my best to rescue those poor little chaps, and do my best to rescue 'em I shall!"

"Yes, Manx, but how?" asked Tom. "If we start a fight over it we'll still be outnumbered, even with you lot here, and then we'll end up as part of the menu ourselves."

"Whatever we do has got to be done quick," said Jack Russell. "There isn't a minute to lose."

"Anyone gotta bit of wire?" asked Scratch.

"There's the radio, or what's left of the radio, lying in yon passage," said Brat Wilson. "Plenty o' wire, there, seesta."

"Good," said Scratch. "Tom, come with me and show me where these rabbits are."

Tom led Scratch, armed with a piece of wire, to the pantry and there Scratch, quickly and professionally, picked the padlock. The poor rabbits, fully convinced that they were about to be eaten, refused to come from the pantry at first, but Tom and Scratch hauled them out, set them on their feet, drove them up the passage to a small rear exit and shoved them, one by one, into the night and freedom. The two cats then returned to H.C. and the rest of the party.

"O.K." said Scratch. "All away."

"But how?" gasped the others.

"One of them little anti-social tricks it's so useful to have up your sleeve sometimes," said Scratch, grinning.

"Wonderful young chap, splendid young chap," chortled old H.C. "Shock some people, no doubt, but there you are. Reminds me so much of my dear friend, O. Slim-Bones. Poor Slim-Bones; he shocked many an old johnny in his time, y'know. He and young Scratch would have made a pair. Remarkable resemblance between 'em. Bit of a rebel in both of 'em, y'know, but it takes a bit of a rebel to make a real cat, eh, what? Never had any time meself for your namby-pamby sort who always toe the line. No need to worry about the future of Catdom while we breed cats like Scratch Sharp!"

"He's a good old stick really," said Scratch to Oliver. "Bit of a fuddy-duddy, but he can't help that. Considering he's nearly old enough to be Father Time in person. Don't know what we'll be like at that age ourselves."

There was a sudden commotion amongst the foxes; they

had discovered that the rabbits were missing. They decided without hesitation that Binks was the guilty party. Binks, protesting, was cuffed and kicked round the cave; Scratch protested. "Look here, the poor little blighter says he never touched 'em; leave it at that, can't you? I mean, we don't need them rabbits to eat, there's bags of food without 'em."

"Always stealing grub, he is," growled Dirky. "Always stealing and stuffing. Come to a sticky end, he will. End up shot as a poultry thief, he will."

The matter was then allowed to drop and the feasting and celebrating began. Toast after toast was drunk, songs were sung, reels and jigs and flings were danced, vows were made of eternal friendship. The merrymaking went on for three days.

Manx Scoop, however, cut his celebrating short in order to go down to Rosthwaite to send further dispatches, taking with him Ranjit Singh. On the evening of the third day they returned, bringing wonderful news; so wonderful he didn't know where to begin, but after some foxglove-brandy to steady his joy-wracked nerves, as he put it, he was able to talk.

"My dispatches have made world-headlines. When they reached my editor, Catdom was about to go into national mourning for you lot; you see. Whiskey Bylines had sent back a story of how all you lot had been eaten by - ahem - aha—Truly good to see you again, Red Rowan. Let's drink to foxes."

They drank to foxes.

"So," continued Manx, "there were pictures of you, splashed all over the front pages, with black frames round them, and all over the country the flags flew at half-mast. Then my dispatches came through; mountain climbed, Expedition safe, everyone alive and kicking, all baloney that you'd been eaten by—aha, yes, yes, it's you, Dirky boy, is it? Delighted, delighted! Let's drink to foxes!"

Again they drank to foxes.

"So," went on Manx, "there was I scooping the world

with this fantastic, terrific, fabulous, glorious victory story. Up went all the flags to the mastheads, day of national thanksgiving announced, pictures of you all on the front pages again, this time with praises and congratulations. And old Whiskey Bylines got the sack from the *Courier*, but the *Evening Blast* has signed him on to cover a story of a pre-historic monster in Ecuador. So off he's gone, with a toothbrush, a typewriter, and three dozen bottles of insect-repellent. At least, that's what they are labelled. Let's drink to Whiskey Bylines. He was a good newspaper-man till he took to hair-restorer, chilblain-lotion and insect-repellent. Stick to honest labels. Let us all drink to honest labels."

"I thought we were drinking to Whiskey Bylines?" asked Felix, laughing.

"Whiskey Bylines, first. Then honest labels," said Manx.

So they drank first to Whiskey Bylines, then to honest labels.

"And," said Manx, "for let us not forget that little word, 'and', without which no page of readable prose could be written. Let us drink to that fine and good and useful little word 'and'."

They drank to the word 'and'.

"So," said Manx. "That is also a good true word. Here is to 'so'."

They drank to 'so'.

"And so," said Manx, "the upshot and outcome of all this is a wonderful, personal message from Her Gracious Majesty, Queen Felicia of the Kingdom of Catland, home of the brave and the free. I have it here. A cablegram; addressed to—let me see, I believe I am holding it upside down. Yes, I am. This foxglove-brandy is a true and straightforward and very powerful drink. Scratch, this cablegram is addressed to you."

Scratch took the cablegram. All the animals mewed and yapped, "Read it to us! Read it!" So Scratch read it to them.

"We are *delighted* by news of your *magnificent* victory stop Please extend to *all* members of the Expedition *including foxes* our *heartiest* congratulations stop Yourself and three summit companions are herewith knighted and *furthermore* awarded the Order of the Grand Solid Gold Cravat, Sword and Sash stop With *sincerest* good wishes and *every hope* for your *swift* and *safe return* stop

Felicia stop

PS Please remember me *particularly* to dear Sir Hywel Catterwaul stop A *most valued* old FRIEND stop"

"Charmin', charmin'!" smirked H.C. "So like her! Personal concern and interest in everythin' she does."

"Grand Solid Gold Cravat, Sword and Sash!" gasped Scratch. "Blimey, but that's the highest honour in Catdom!"

"Bravo, Sir Scratch, likewise Sir Oliver, Sir Red Rowan and Sir Hamish!" cried Manx. "Let us drink to these four knights!"

So everyone drank.

"And now, Sir Knights," said Manx, "a short interview to register your first reactions to these tremendous honours. Scratch, how d'you feel about all this?"

"Dead chuffed," said Scratch.

"Same here," said Oliver.

Hamish sighed, "Jings! Words fail me!"

Red Rowan said slowly, "Well, it's a rare honour, like, for a fox."

Next day all the Expedition animals went down to Base Camp to prepare for departure from the mountain and their return to the capital of Catdom, where they would receive a Royal welcome and attend a special investiture and banquet at the Palace.

Red Rowan was to travel back with them, of course, and Wee Hamish, too.

It was arranged that Red Rowan (who pleaded a few odd jobs to attend to before departure, including equipping himself with something in the way of decent clothes) should join them at Base Camp. But although the other animals waited for him there long after the appointed hour, no Red Rowan turned up. The animals became impatient and anxious; there were airplanes waiting at Penrith to fly them home.

Then, when they had given up all hope of the fox, they saw two little red figures slithering and skipping down the mountainside. Binks and Benn.

"Missage," said Binks. "Missage from Red Rowan."

"Sir Red Rowan, young fellamelad," said H.C.

"Red Rowan says," recited Binks, who had clearly learned this by heart, "Red Rowan says he's verra grateful to yon Queen for sirring him and giving him yon crav – cra – vat an' that, but he's a fox and us foxes can have no truck with sirrings and cravs – cravats an' sashes an' sic like. So he thanks Her Majesty reet weel, but begs to remain plain meester."

"But he can't turn down an honour like that! The biggest honour in Catdom!" exclaimed H.C.

"Begs to remain plain meester," repeated Binks.

"Aye," said Benn.

There was a long pause. Then Scratch said, "Well, I can see his point. And if that's how he feels that's how he feels. But it's a real pity, for I was looking forward to having him at the Palace with us. It won't be the same without old Red."

"Once a fox, always a fox," said H.C. "A rum lot."

There was another pause. Then Binks said, "Have you owt for a young chap to eat, like?"

So they gave the cubs some Kendal Mint Cake and then Binks and Benn said good-bye with their mouths full and ran back up the mountain.

"We might as well start going down now," said Scratch sadly. The other animals agreed. "Let's go then," said Scratch.

One by one they filed away from the empty camp-site by the tarn, Scratch bringing up the rear. He looked round for the last time: the tarn with its rocks and iron-grey water, the marks where the tents had stood on the green turf, the steep crag-broken mountainside swinging upward into a curtain of cloud. So he stood looking; saying good-bye to it all.

Then, from somewhere above, came a sharp yappitty-yap-yap in a well-known voice. Scratch straightened, his heart rose, he looked up, hoping for the lithe, dancing red silhouette. But all was still, vacant, silent. The cloud blew lower, the tarn trembled as a wind-gust crossed it. Scratch sighed, grinned sadly, shook his head, muttered, "So long, old Red." He slowly followed the rest of his party into the ravine.